The Anti-Princess Club
CRUISE CONTROL

SAMANTHA TURNBULL
ILLUSTRATED by
SARAH DAVIS

ALLEN&UNWIN
SYDNEY • MELBOURNE • AUCKLAND • LONDON

First published by Allen & Unwin in 2015

Allen & Unwin – Australia
83 Alexander Street, Crows Nest NSW 2065, Australia
Phone: (61 2) 8425 0100
Email: info@allenandunwin.com
Web: www.allenandunwin.com

Allen & Unwin – UK
c/o Murdoch Books, Erico House, 93-99 Upper Richmond Road,
London SW15 2TG, UK
Phone: (44 20) 8785 5995
Email: info@murdochbooks.co.uk
Web: www.allenandunwin.com
Murdoch Books is a wholly owned division of Allen & Unwin Pty Ltd

A Cataloguing-in-Publication entry is available from the
National Library of Australia
www.trove.nla.gov.au.
A catalogue record for this book is available from the British Library

ISBN (AUS) 978 1 76029 188 4
ISBN (UK) 978 1 74336 807 7

Cover and text design by Vida & Luke Kelly
Set in 13pt Fairfield LT Std, Light
This book was printed in September 2015 by McPherson's Printing Group, Australia.

1 3 5 7 9 10 8 6 4 2

The paper in this book is FSC® certified.
FSC® promotes environmentally responsible, socially beneficial and economically viable management of the world's forests.

For all of my strong,
smart and supportive
Northern Star women

MAZE BREAK AUSTRALIA

MEMBERS ONLINE: 112 **MODERATOR:** Billy27

Maze Break Leaderboard:

1. Jake_can_break17
2. Skywalker2000
3. Ironman13
4. Xavier111
5. Justice4all
6. Will_will_will
7. MaXiMuS
8. Ant16
9. AP23
10. Lin2win

Congratulations, Maze Breakers! If your username appears on the leaderboard you need to check your emails – STAT!

'Eeeeeeee!'

My squeal scares Dad into dropping a cereal box on the kitchen floor. He looks like a human island in a sea of rice bubbles – I'd guess around 550 of the crunchy little suckers. I counted every rice bubble in an entire box once – there were 1016.

'Sorry, Dad,' I say. 'I'll sweep them up for you in forty-seven seconds.'

I was trying to sneak in a game of Maze Break on my laptop during breakfast, but now I've blown my cover.

'That doesn't look like homework,' Dad says.

'Maze Break may as well be homework. Most kids could learn some pretty sweet maths skills if they played it too,' I say. 'Anyway, this pop-up says I'm on the Maze Break leaderboard. Look at the list – I'm placed ninth!'

In Maze Break, players have to race through mazes and crack codes or solve equations at the end before they can progress to the next level. Times are recorded and the fastest make the leaderboard.

I've never made the top ten, so this is a BIG deal.

Dad raises one eyebrow until it almost blends in with his hair – it's a freaky facial manoeuvre I've been trying to master. 'I thought your mum and I said you weren't allowed to chat on that thing.'

I minimise the web page and swivel my stool around to face him. 'I'm not chatting to any players, Dad. It's a pop-up message from the Maze Break administrators.'

I actually know a whole lot more about technology than Mum or Dad, but I follow their rules when it comes to online stuff. It's all basic Cyber-Safety 101.

Maze Break only came out at the start of this year. My parents had to give me special permission to sign up because it's recommended for kids over twelve (I've just turned eleven). And they only let me play on the following conditions:

1) I have the chat function disabled (in case any weirdo strangers try to strike up a conversation).
2) I limit my playing time to half an hour per day (which is lucky for the other Maze Breakers, as otherwise I'd probably be in the number one spot on the leaderboard).
3) I don't use my real name or age (I'm AP23).

My real name is Emily Martin. AP stands for anti-princess. I'm the president of the Anti-Princess Club – my three best friends and I started the club because we were sick of everyone treating us like helpless damsels in distress.

I tacked 23 on the end of my username because it's my favourite number. It's the smallest prime number made up of two consecutive prime numbers. I'm a numbers nerd, or maths genius if you want to put it a little more politely.

'Well, AP23,' Dad says, 'better check your emails – maybe you've won a million dollars!'

I open my inbox and see four new emails.

Three are from the other founding members of the Anti-Princess Club: Bella Singh, Grace Bennett and Chloe Karalis.

But the email at the top is the one Dad and I are interested in right now.

TO: AP23

FROM: Maze Break

SUBJECT: Top 10 Summer Showdown

Congratulations, AP23!

You've beaten 7163 players to make the coveted Maze Break Australian leaderboard.

To celebrate your achievement, as well as Maze Break's first birthday, we're offering you a once-in-a-lifetime opportunity.

The Maze Break Summer Showdown will be held aboard the cruise ship *Capricorn Princess.*

You and three others (including at least one parent or guardian for Maze Breakers under 18) will board the ship at Fremantle, Western Australia (flights to Perth for Maze Breakers outside of WA are included in the prize).

You will spend nine days cruising through the Indian Ocean, with stops at Geraldton and Exmouth, before participating in the Maze Break Summer Showdown.

To claim your prize and for further details please phone Maze Break HQ on 02 5550 7843.

Yours in gaming,
Maze Break creator Billy27

'What's left you two speechless?' Mum asks.

Dad and I didn't notice her and my little sister Ava walk into the kitchen. And it's a wonder we haven't caught any bugs in our mouths with the way they're gaping open.

'Emily's won a cruise,' Dad says. 'It leaves in just over a month.'

Mum starts sweeping up the rice bubbles. 'It must be spam,' she says. 'I get emails like that all the time.'

Ava shudders. 'Yuck. Boats make me spew.'

Mum frowns at Ava. She doesn't like the word 'spew'. She says 'be sick' is a lady-like alternative. I say 'spew' all the time.

Dad unclips his mobile from his belt and starts jabbing buttons.

I skim the words again. 'It's a once-in-a-lifetime opportunity,' I repeat out loud.

Dad clears his throat. 'Yes, hello. This is Corporal Leo Martin, the father of Emily Martin.'

Dad's in the Army, but he doesn't usually introduce himself with his rank. He must want to sound official.

'AP23 is her username...She's eleven...Yes, it is young...She was playing with our consent... Yes, I'm her guardian...I'm calling to confirm the authenticity of this morning's email...So, it's real?...We're in Newcastle – New South Wales...So, we'd fly out the morning of the cruise? Leaving Sydney at 5am?...Four tickets? ...Thank you. Thank you very much.'

Dad turns to me with a smile like an upside-down taco. 'Looks like we're going on a cruise!' he shouts.

I jump to my feet and throw my arms around Dad.

'How about it, Lesley?' he asks Mum. 'We could use a family holiday, don't you think?'

Mum empties the dustpan of rice bubbles into the bin and closes the lid with a sigh. 'I can't go,' she says. 'It's my busiest time of year in the salon. I'm already booked out.'

Mum's a beautician. She runs her own business from home.

'And I'd need a spew bucket,' Ava says. 'I'd rather help Mum pop pimples.'

I giggle at the thought of a six-year-old assistant beautician.

'Come on, love,' Dad says to Mum. 'Couldn't you shut down for a week? Take an early Christmas? We could feed Ava ginger – I've heard it helps with nausea.'

Mum shakes her head firmly. 'It's just the wrong time of year for me,' she says. 'Everyone wants to look good for their Christmas parties. It's all locked in, Leo.'

'Don't make me do it, Dad,' Ava says, putting her hands on her tummy. 'Remember when we went whale watching last year? I spewed all over the captain.'

Dad slumps down on a stool. 'I guess you'll have to invite your anti-princess mates, Emily,' he says. 'We'll have two tickets left over.'

Now it's my turn to slump. 'Dad, there are three of them,' I say. 'You know I couldn't leave one out.'

Dad knows Bella, Grace and Chloe have been my best friends since kindergarten. After this summer, we'll be into our last year of primary school ever.

'Why don't you see what their folks reckon?' he says. 'If they're all on board, I'll just have to treat myself to an extra ticket.'

Before Dad has even finished his sentence, I've started typing.

Bella, Grace, Chloe

APC meeting needed ASAP. Treehouse, today?

Emily

I lift a corner of the rug on the treehouse floor and kick a chocolate wrapper and some dirt underneath. Cleaning is not my strong suit.

When I grow up I want to design and build a bunch of different houses, but as for the cleaning – no thanks. Maybe I'll hire my brother Max as a maid. I already pay him a few dollars here and there to tidy the treehouse. He's earning big money for a nine-year-old.

'Bella, you there?' Emily calls from the bottom of the ladder.

I stick my head out the window and wave. 'Come on up!'

Emily has called an urgent meeting of the Anti-Princess Club. Our treehouse HQ, designed and built by me, is in my backyard, so I'm always first here.

'Why did you want to meet today instead of at school tomorrow?' I ask as Emily reaches the top rung.

She puts her laptop bag down and grins. 'Just you wait,' she says. 'I want Grace and Chloe here too before I reveal all.'

As if on cue, two voices echo across the yard.

'Wait up, Grace!' Chloe yells.

'You hurry up, Chloe!' Grace calls back.

Grace gets to the tree first and appears at the doorway within seconds. Chloe's not far behind, puffing a little after trying to keep up with Grace.

'What's this about?' Grace asks.

We all look at Emily, who is bringing up something on her laptop. She flips it around so the screen is facing us.

'It's a photo of a ship,' I say. 'Now that's something I'd like to design. It would have a glass bottom so you could see all the fish underneath your feet. It would have a flying fox to take you from bow to stern. There'd be a rooftop garden…no, an actual forest—'

Chloe cuts me off. 'You can re-enter design-mode in a minute, Bella,' she says. 'Let Emily explain why she's showing us a ship.'

Emily claps her hands and starts to bounce with excitement. 'I won a cruise!' she yells. 'And you're all invited! I have four tickets… well, Dad is buying one for himself so you can all come too. It's next month, the week after school finishes…in Western Australia!'

I blink as I try to snap out of imagining my own cruise ship design. 'A cruise?' I ask. 'Like a holiday on a ship?'

Emily nods and claps again.

'But how?' Grace asks.

Emily brings up another web page.

'Is that Maze Break?' Chloe asks. 'I'm not very good at that. You've got to be so fast.'

Emily can't contain herself. She jumps to her feet and squeals: 'Exactly! And I'm in the top ten fastest Maze Breakers in Australia!

We're all being flown to Perth to go on a cruise where we'll race against each other in the Maze Break Summer Showdown! It's a once-in-a-lifetime opportunity!'

I can't believe my ears. 'Who wins a holiday for playing a computer game?' I ask.

Emily stops bouncing. 'Don't you believe me?' she asks.

I've never been on a cruise. In fact, I've never been to the west coast.

'Of course I believe you – and, yes, I want to come!' I squeal.

Chloe jumps up from the floor and hugs Emily. 'Me too!' she says.

Grace inhales slowly. 'Will your parents let you go?' she asks. 'I don't think mine will. They don't have much cash around Christmas time.'

I know my parents will be on board – not on board the ship, but on board with the idea. They love Emily's dad and are always looking for creative babysitting options. Mum and

Dad are both super busy doctors, so Max and I get babysat a lot.

'I think mine will be fine,' Chloe says. 'Yiayia will miss me, of course.'

Emily types something on her laptop.

'Here, Grace,' she says. 'I'm emailing you all the terms and conditions so you can show your parents. It's an all-expenses-paid trip – from the flight to Perth, to the cruise, to the food and activities. They've got to let you come.'

Grace manages a small smile. 'I don't want to get my hopes up,' she says. 'I'll have to wait and see.'

Emily raises her arms towards the tree-house ceiling – it's a geodesic dome, the treehouse doubles as a planetarium I designed myself.

'Ahoy, me hearties!' she yells. 'The anti-princesses are about to sail the seven seas!'

Emily pauses. I can guess what she's about to say next – these maths types can't cope with inaccuracies.

'Well, technically, we'll only be sailing one sea,' she says. 'Seven just sounds good. I don't know why everyone likes seven so much, but there are seven wonders of the world, seven days in the week, seven basic musical notes…'

I zone out and go back to designing my own cruise ship in my head. Maybe it can have seven floors.

CHAPTER THREE

Deep breath in. Deep breath out. Deep breath in. Out. In. Out.

I'm trying to stop myself from hyperventilating as Dad finishes reading Emily's email.

Dad hands the tablet to Mum so she can read it too.

'I think it sounds great,' he says. 'We'll have to chat to Emily's parents about it, but it all looks good on paper, and you'll be back in time for Christmas.'

I close my eyes. 'Oh,' I say.

'Oh?' Dad asks. 'You're not happy that I'm willing to let you go to the other side of the country for the first nine days of the school holidays with your friends?'

Mum looks up from the tablet. 'Don't you want to go?' she asks.

I shrug. I didn't want to kill the excitement in the treehouse when Emily told everyone about the cruise. It would be awesome to be with my friends, but the truth is I couldn't think of anything worse than being cooped up in one place for nine days straight.

'When Emily said the words "cruise ship" I panicked a bit,' I say. 'No sports fields, no grass, nowhere to run around. It's not my thing.'

Mum shuffles her chair over to mine and opens the cruise ship company's website.

'Let's have a look at the ship together,' she says. 'I think you'll be surprised by what's on offer for active people. Your father and I went on one before you, Tom, Oliver and Harry were born, and there was lots to do.'

Dad huddles in behind us as Mum clicks on a link that says 'Things to Do'.

> DINING

> ENTERTAINMENT

> RELAXATION

> SPORTS

'Click on sports!' I say.

A new list pops up.

ONBOARD ACTIVITIES:

- Three swimming pools
- Waterslide
- Basketball court
- Putt-putt golf
- Two gymnasiums
- Table tennis
- Rock climbing wall

ACTIVITIES AT PORTS OF CALL:

- Beach volleyball
- Fishing
- Snorkelling
- Scuba diving
- Sailing

I take the tablet from Mum's hands and click on 'sailing'.

The Capricorn Princess *docks at Exmouth on Day Six of the cruise, where passengers can take part in a mini regatta.*

'I am SO going to win this sailing competition,' I say. 'I'll have to practise on one of those hire boats down at the lake.'

Dad laughs. 'Well, that didn't take much effort,' he says. 'Shall I call Emily's parents now and tell them you're in?'

I nod without looking up from the tablet. 'I've got four weeks,' I say. 'I reckon that's enough time for me to reach skipper-status.'

I type 'sailing for beginners' into the browser as Dad talks on the telephone.

'So, all the girls are going?' he asks. 'That's great. Yep, we're fine with Grace coming along – thanks so much for giving her the chance, it really is a once-in-a-lifetime opportunity…'

Dear Yiayia,

I'm going to miss you so much. I wish the cruise included free tickets for grandmothers.

Don't worry – nine days will go so fast. I'll be back before you know it.

At least Alex will be back from boarding school to keep you company – I've told him to make you lots of tea while I'm gone.

I thought I'd leave you with a new version of our rizogalo recipe. I know rizogalo was your favourite dessert when you were growing up in Greece, but last time we cooked it together you said it tasted a bit plain. I've been experimenting with replacing the cornflour with almond meal and the vanilla essence with almond extract.

If you get bored without me there, maybe you can whip up a batch and let me know how it goes!

See you soon,

Chloe xxx

Dear Yiayia

Chloe's Rizogalo

Ingredients: 100g white rice, 500ml water, 500ml full cream milk, 4 tablespoons caster sugar, 150ml cream, 4 tablespoons almond meal, 2 teaspoons almond extract. Garnish: a few pinches ground cinnamon and a small handful of ground almonds.

Method: Bring rice and water to boil in a saucepan then immediately turn heat to low. Simmer, stirring occasionally for about half an hour until the rice is soft and has absorbed most of the water.

Add the milk and sugar and bring to the boil. Mix cream and almond meal then add to boiling rice mixture in saucepan. Add almond extract and stir. Remove from stove, pour into bowl and allow to cool to room temperature. Sprinkle with cinnamon and almonds and chill in fridge for at least three hours.

'S'agapo,' Yiayia says.

'I love you too, Yiayia,' I say.

Emily's dad is showing the rest of our parents a diagram of the ship.

'The girls are in a four-berth room with a porthole,' he says. 'I've got a single interior suite across the hall, so no window for me.'

Mum squeezes my shoulders. 'You be careful on that thing,' she says. 'You ask Mr Martin to show you where the lifejackets are straight away, okay? And the lifeboats.'

Emily's dad winks at Mum. 'If the ship runs into trouble, I'll be the one looking to these girls for help,' he says. 'You know they don't need rescuing.'

We all laugh at the mention of the Anti-Princess Club motto. We came up with 'we don't need rescuing' because we thought it was lame how so many princesses need rescuing by princes in fairytales. In fact, we call them *unfair*ytales.

An announcement comes over the airport loudspeakers: *Attention passengers, Flight 1279 to Perth is now open for boarding. Please make your way to Gate 23.*

Emily claps with excitement. 'Twenty-three!

My lucky number. Well, not that mathematicians believe in luck, but it is a cool coincidence.'

The mums and dads erupt into last-minute checks and warnings.

'Have you got enough sunscreen?' Emily's mum asks.

'Be careful the deck isn't too slippery if you go jogging,' Grace's dad says.

'Don't hesitate to call me, I'll have my pager,' Bella's mum says.

'Eat some extra dessert for me,' Yiayia says.

I wave my index finger at her. 'Don't think you can go crazy with sweets while I'm gone,' I say. 'Your blood sugar levels need to stay stable.'

Yiayia was diagnosed with type 2 diabetes earlier this year. It's one of my many scientific dreams to find a cure.

'Okay, girls.' Emily's dad picks up his carry-on luggage. 'Let's fly.'

Mum twists her hair nervously. 'Are you sure you'll be okay?' she asks.

Another plane takes off just outside a window nearby, distracting me as I kiss Mum goodbye.

'How do they do that?' I overhear a little boy ask a man a few metres away.

I can't help myself. 'It's physics,' I answer. 'Thrust and lift are the forces that keep a plane in the air. Thrust comes from the engine and lift comes from the design of the plane itself.'

Dad takes Mum by the hand and waves me off. 'They'll be fine,' he says. 'By this afternoon they'll be steering the ship themselves.'

The *Capricorn Princess* is casting a massive shadow across the crowd gathered at the harbour.

'Why would they name a giant ship after a princess?' I ask. 'Let's hope it doesn't need rescuing at sea.'

A woman wearing a white suit turns and smiles at me. 'That's a good question,' she says. 'It doesn't seem to fit, does it? My last ship was called the *Atlantic Warrior*, which I didn't think was a great name either – doesn't sound very relaxing.'

A man in a blue shirt that says *Capricorn Princess* across the back hands the woman a white hat with a gold rope strap around the middle and a black visor.

'Here you go, captain,' he says. 'Time to head up.'

She pulls it onto her head before nodding at us and walking away.

Dad gives me a nudge in the ribs. 'Looks like you just met the most important person on the ship,' he says. 'Luckily you didn't offend her with the anti-princess jibe.'

Two more men in *Capricorn Princess* shirts point at the pink lanyards around our necks. They came with our tickets and say MB VIP. It doesn't take a genius to crack that acronym – Maze Break Very Important Person.

'I see you're a Maze Breaker,' one of the men says to Dad. 'If you could head over to the other end of the harbour, that's where all the gamers and their families are congregating. You'll be boarding first.'

Dad pushes our luggage trolley towards the ship's bow. I do a quick head count of the lanyard-wearers. Forty-one, including us. I try to pinpoint the actual Maze Breakers among the families and friends.

There's a girl about my age playing with a mobile phone.

'Dad, I can't work this thing!' she yells. 'How do you download an app?'

I scratch her from the possibilities. A Maze Breaker would know how to download an app.

A group of five boys in their teens seems to be separating from the rest. 'You should go over and introduce yourself, Emily,' Grace says.

I'm about to follow her suggestion when another teenage boy approaches us. He's hard to miss with his blue mohawk slicked into a spiky peak in the middle of his head.

He speaks directly to Dad. 'I'm Maximus,' he says. 'Just sussing out who's who, and I think I've got it narrowed down now. Are you Justice4all, Jake_can_break17 or AP23? I've already met a couple of the others like Ironman and Will in the chatroom, but AP23 and Jake are a bit mysterious. Jake's the top of the leaderboard, so I figure it's part of his game plan to stay quiet. I didn't expect you to be so old. How old are you? Do you play anything else online? Zombie Spat? Hammer Man?'

Dad's mouth is opening and closing like a fish's as he 'ums' and 'ahs' trying to answer Maximus's machine-gun questions. 'Zombie what?' he manages.

I step in front of Dad, but Maximus speaks over the top of me. 'What an awesome dad you've got. I bet you'll be cheering him on at the showdown.' He waves at someone behind Dad. 'Gotta go. I've just spotted Xavier. See you on the ship!'

Bella, Grace and Chloe scrunch up their noses as we watch Maximus bop away towards the next gamer.

'As if your dad is the Maze Breaker,' Bella says. 'Why would he think that?'

Grace looks at Maximus, then back at the other teenagers talking among themselves. 'Well, they're all guys,' she says. 'And we're only eleven. They all look like teenagers.'

Dad puffs out his chest. 'So, I look like a teenager,' he says.

I roll my eyes. 'He said that you looked old, Dad,' I say. 'Not that he let you get a word in.' I fold my arms and start counting the rows of portholes on the ships to calm myself down.

'Don't worry, Emily,' Chloe says. 'It's just that your username doesn't give away your age, or that you're a girl. We can set them straight.'

I stop counting. 'Oh, we won't be setting them straight,' I say. 'Let them think Dad is a Maze Breaker. The joke will be on them.'

I snatch a pen sticking out of Chloe's backpack and write on the back of my lanyard.

Mission Maze Break: Reveal the real AP23 at the Top Ten Summer Showdown – and win

I show Grace, Bella and Chloe. 'All in favour?'

They raise their hands.

Our bathroom is so tiny that you could sit on the toilet while having a shower.

'It's a toiwer, or is it a showet?' I say. 'Why waste time pooing then showering when you could do both at once?'

Grace giggles, then breathes onto the porthole glass and wipes it with her sleeve. 'I can't see land anymore,' she says. 'Nothing but blue sea and blue sky.'

I peer over her shoulder. 'I can handle the small bathroom,' I say. 'But if I was the ship designer I definitely would've made that a bigger window.'

Emily unfolds a map of the ship and lays it out on one of the bottom bunks. 'Dad says we can have an hour to explore,' she says. 'Can you believe they have six restaurants on this thing? And two shops – a gift shop and a general store.'

Chloe pulls her wallet out of her suitcase. 'Let's go look,' she says. 'I wouldn't mind getting some chocolate from that general store...just so we have a stash.'

Chloe doesn't need to say 'chocolate' twice. It's the anti-princesses' favourite food. I keep at least a dozen bars in the treehouse at all times.

Grace leads the way up four flights of stairs to the main deck. Everyone, except Grace, is puffing a little at the top.

'I wonder if any cruise ships have lifts,' I say. 'I'll put a couple in mine when I design it.'

Grace bends her knee into a calf stretch. 'There actually is a lift here,' she says. 'I didn't want to tell you, because I can't think of anything worse – it would be like being stuck inside a box inside another box.'

'Good point,' I say. 'I'll make sure the lifts

I design are nice and roomy – so outdoor types like you are comfy.'

Emily scratches her chin – she does that when she's thinking. 'The general store is starboard way,' she says. 'That's the right side when we're facing forward towards the bow.'

We weave through about fifty sunlounges.

'Hey, there it is!' Chloe calls out. She's pointing at a sign that says *General Store* in green and yellow lettering alongside a pineapple. Next door to that it says *Gift Shop* in flashing neon lights.

'You guys get the chocolates,' I say. 'I'll have a browse around the gift shop. I told Max I'd get him something.'

The other anti-princesses disappear through the glass doors as I head to the gift shop.

I stop in front of the main window display.

There are rows upon rows of dolls in grass skirts, leis and sequined crop tops. They all have long blonde hair, light brown skin and enormous empty eyes.

'How unique,' I whisper sarcastically.

I step inside the shop and see a man pull a twenty-dollar note from his pocket as his daughter clutches one of the dolls.

'Are these the only dolls you have?' the girl asks the man behind the counter.

'Yes, they are,' he says.

I turn back to the window display and do a quick count of the little blonde heads. Emily would've been more precise, but I guess there are about a hundred dolls taking up far more space than any other product in the shop.

I browse the other shelves for something for Max. There's a model cruise ship, Hawaiian shirts, stuffed toy sharks and turtles.

Nothing grabs my attention, so I head back outside. Emily, Chloe and Grace are waiting for me with chocolate supplies.

'Check out those dolls,' Chloe says. 'They look kind of creepy.'

I give them one last glance. 'They do, don't they?'

Phwweeeeeeet.

A woman in white shorts and a blue *Capricorn Princess* shirt blows the whistle around her neck.

'Welcome aboard!' she yells. 'I trust you've all found your sea legs after your first night on the open ocean. My name is Kate Donaldson and I'm the *Capricorn Princess's* director of sports. You'll see I've put some posters and sign-up sheets on the wall here with different headings. They represent all the sporting activities you can take part in throughout the cruise – everything from basketball to rock climbing and our mini sailing regatta.'

I clap at the mention of the regatta.

'The sign-up sheets are over here,' Kate says. 'So take your time, and write your name under any of the activities that take your fancy.'

Emily's dad makes a beeline for the fishing poster.

I head to the poster that says *Sailing*.

The mini-regatta will take place on Day 6 of the cruise when the Capricorn Princess *docks at Exmouth. Sailors will compete in crews of two on double-handed dinghies.*

Emily, Bella and Chloe hover around me.

'Crews of two,' I say. 'That's interesting – I've only ever sailed a one-person dinghy.'

Chloe takes a marker and signs her name on the snorkelling poster.

'You all in?' she asks. 'It says the first snorkelling session is on tomorrow.'

Everyone nods, so she adds our names.

'Do I have a volunteer to join me in my sailing pair?' I ask.

I don't have a preference for my partner. Emily is a natural leader and would make a great navigator, Bella knows the mechanics of how to steer anything (she almost won a billycart derby earlier this year), and Chloe's scientific brain would come in handy for picking wind direction and understanding the physics of how to sail with speed.

'I'll do it!' Emily says. 'A bit of competition will get me fired up for the Maze Break showdown!'

'Awesome,' I say. 'I hereby propose a mission to win the regatta!'

Emily grabs a marker from underneath one of the posters and pulls a notepad from her pocket.

She holds up the page for us to inspect:

Mission Set Sail: Team Anti-Princess win the mini-regatta

'All in favour?' Emily asks.

Bella, Chloe and I raise our hands.

I take the marker from Emily and sign us up on the sailing poster:

Team Anti-Princess

Dear Yiayia,

The cruise is awesome so far, but I wish you were here too.

On the first day, we explored the ship (it's **HUGE**) and had burgers for dinner (no Greek restaurants on board).

Yesterday we signed up for a bunch of activities. Grace and Emily are going in a sailing race, Mr Martin's going fishing and we're all heading out snorkelling today when we stop at Geraldton.

I cant wait to head out to Ningaloo Reef – **MARINE BIOLOGY CENTRAL!**

The photo on the front is a Caretta caretta. They're an endangered sea turtle – the crew says we might see one at Ningaloo.

Have you tried the rizogalo recipe yet?

Love, Chloe xxx

I hand Yiayia's postcard to a crew member collecting mail.

I see it as soon as my feet hit the dock.

'Over there!' I yell.

An elderly man in bright white sneakers steps on the back of one of my thongs. 'What's the hold-up?'

I push my glasses up the bridge of my nose and squint at the harbour's green water. 'There,' I say. 'About ten metres away. It's a turtle!'

Everyone on the dock turns at once. Some pull out their cameras, others bend down to try to get a closer look.

The crew member who was collecting our mail stops by my side and frowns at the black circle. Her name badge says *Marnie*.

'Something's not right,' she says.

The turtle is floating but not swimming.

Marnie pulls out her phone and scrolls through her contacts.

'What species do you think it is, Chloe?' Grace asks.

I squint at the shell as the waves gently rock it from side to side. Part of me wants to jump off the dock and swim straight to it. If only they'd handed out the snorkelling gear already.

'There are four types of turtle it could be,' I say. 'A hawksbill, a green turtle, a flatback or a loggerhead. It's not very big, but its head looks quite large. It could be a *Caretta caretta* – sorry, a loggerhead. A baby, maybe.'

Marnie is speaking to someone on the phone. 'It's definitely sick or injured…We're in Geraldton – in the harbour…I know you're at Exmouth, but isn't there someone we can call here?…I can't leave the passengers now to go searching for another vet…We dock at Exmouth on Thursday…All right, but I won't have time to care for it on board…Okay, see you Thursday.'

Marnie paces back to the ship and I follow without bothering to ask Mr Martin.

'Chloe!' Bella calls.

'We're coming with you!' Emily shouts.

I jog to catch up to Marnie.

'Excuse me, but who was that on the phone?' I ask. 'Are we rescuing the turtle ourselves?'

Marnie strides up the gangplank with her head down.

'It was Dr Meyer,' she says. 'She's a vet I know who specialises in injured turtles. She's in Exmouth and that's where we stop on Thursday, so it looks like we're taking a special passenger.'

Marnie opens a cupboard and pulls out a long-handled fishing net. She marches back down the gangplank and around the dock.

'That turtle is going to need to be kept moist,' I say. I pull a couple of beach towels from the bag we packed to go snorkelling. 'Grace, can you wet these?'

The dock is too high to dangle the towels in the sea, so Grace runs to a tap and starts to drench them under the water.

'The turtle might be too heavy for me to lift,' Marnie says, 'so I'm going to use the net to guide it over there.'

She points to a ramp from the sea to the top of the dock.

'Everyone move!' I call out.

There are about fifty people taking photos and filming us with their phones.

'We need some space on the dock to guide the turtle to the ramp!' I yell again.

Emily, Bella and Mr Martin herd the crowd away so the space is clear for Marnie and me.

'Easy, little fella,' Marnie says as she scoops the turtle into the net. She keeps the net submerged with the turtle inside and heads towards the ramp.

I grab the end of the net's handle as well and help Marnie pull against the water.

We take long, slow steps until we reach the base of the ramp.

'What's your name?' Marnie asks.

'Chloe.'

'Well, Chloe, I want you to keep hold of the handle as I lower myself down the ramp to help our little friend up, okay?'

I nod and plant my feet firmly on the dock.

Marnie slides down the ramp and pulls the turtle from the net. 'He's actually pretty light!' she calls out. 'Must be a juvenile.'

She cradles the shell under one arm like a football and crawls back up to the dock.

Grace hands me the dripping towels and I wrap the turtle up.

'I'm not sure if he's alive,' Marnie says. 'Maybe he's sleeping.'

I remember watching a documentary about turtle rescues. 'I know how to tell,' I say.

I gently stroke the turtle's eyelids. Emily, Bella and Grace gather in close to see if there's a reaction.

'Look,' Bella whispers. 'He's opening his eyes.'

'How do you know it's a he?' Emily asks.

I look for the tail. 'We don't yet,' I say. 'You can't tell with loggerheads until they're adults. Males have thicker tails and shorter plastrons than females – the plastron is the flat belly part of the shell.'

Another crew member arrives and taps Mr Martin on the back.

'Excuse me, sir, but if your group wants to come snorkelling it's time to go,' he says. 'There's a bus waiting on the other side of the harbour to take us to the beach.'

Emily shakes her head at her dad.

'Looks like the girls have other priorities,' he says. 'We'll have to wait for the snorkelling at Exmouth.'

Marnie wipes her brow with her forearm. 'You know a lot about turtles, Chloe,' she says. 'Any idea what I'm supposed to do with it for the next few days?'

The turtle opens its eyes once more and looks directly into mine.

'Leave it to me,' I say. 'I'll take care of it.'

MAZE BREAK CHATROOM

MEMBERS ONLINE: 3 **MODERATOR:** Billy27

Jake_can_break17 is online.

Xavier111 is online.

MaXiMus is online.

'Dad, can I turn the chat function on?' I ask. 'I just want to see what the others are saying.'

Dad makes a 'hmmmmmm' sound. 'I guess it's okay while I'm here,' he says. 'But don't complain if I'm snooping behind you looking at the screen. I've heard about cyber bullies, you know.'

'Thanks, Dad.'

AP23 is online.

I figured it was a good time to grab a bit of Maze Break practice in Dad's suite since we're not snorkelling and Chloe, Bella and Grace are busy fussing over the turtle.

XAVIER111: AP23, I don't think I've seen you with chat turned on before. Welcome.

MAXIMUS: Yo, AP, where are you? Xavier and I are on our laptops near the waterslide. You should come join us.

I stick to my word to Dad and don't reply.

XAVIER111: Gone all shy?

MAXIMUS: I told you he's trying to be mysterious – like Jake_can_break17

XAVIER111: Hey AP, MaXiMus says you look more like 50 than 23 – how old are you anyway?

I try to hide a giggle, but my snorting makes Dad glance at the screen. 'Hey,' he says. 'Tell those guys to give me a break.'

'You mean I can reply to them?' I ask.

Dad scratches his chin. He does that when he's thinking – it's a family trait.

'Okay,' he says. 'But only because I'm right here.'

I try to speak like Dad.

AP23: Hey guys, give me a break.

XAVIER111: He speaks!!

MAXIMUS: He cracked!

AP23: I know we're not the same age, but I have every right to be here, OK?

XAVIER111: We were just kidding, AP.

MAXIMUS: All good, AP23.

I turn the chat function off and start a proper game of Maze Break.

My avatar pops up on screen – you get to choose from a list of animals when you sign up. Everyone else chose dangerous creatures like cobras, tigers and wolves, but I chose a pigeon. Chloe told me a scientist once did an experiment to test the knowledge of pigeons and their mathematical skills were just as impressive as a monkey's. One pigeon could even place the numbers one to five in order.

I move my pigeon through the latest maze as quickly as I can, taking note of the dead ends so I don't run into them a second time.

'That's just like Pac-Man,' Dad says.

'It's nothing like Pac-Man,' I say.

I consider shutting the computer down so I can focus on arguing with Dad, but I suppose it's good practice to try to concentrate on the game while speaking. You never know what pressure we'll be put under in the actual showdown on Sunday.

'Pac-Man ate things and had enemies trying to catch him,' I continue. 'Maze Break is just you, the clock and your brain. You have to get to the end of the maze as fast as you can on your own, then you have to solve a mathematical problem to get to the next level.'

Dad yawns. 'Sounds a bit boring to me,' he says. 'No monsters or fighting. What happens when you finish the whole thing?'

I press pause.

'Finish the whole thing?' I repeat. 'I don't know if there is a finish. I figured the developers would keep building mazes as long as someone was willing to break them.'

Dad yawns again and lies down on his bunk.

'That sounds tiring,' he says. 'I'm going to catch some zeds. Shut the door quietly when you head back to your room, okay?'

I restart the game and play for a few more minutes.

Hunghk, shhhhh. Hunnnnnghk, shhhhhh. Hunnnngggkkkk, ssshhhhhh.

I watch Dad's shoulders rise and fall as he snores.

'Should I?' I whisper.

I pull up the chatroom again.

Jake_can_break17 is online.

Xavier111 is online.

MaXiMus is online.

I take another look at Dad, then press the enter key.

AP23 is online.

XAVIER111: He's back!

AP23: Just a quick question.

XAVIER111: Shoot.

AP23: Is there an end to Maze Break? You know... like a final level eventually?

MAXIMUS: I don't know for sure, but I figure there will be. Nothing lasts forever.

XAVIER111: My theory is that they'll have annual showdowns for five or ten years, then have some major end-of-game-forever showdown.

AP23: Right.

JAKE_CAN_BREAK17: No.

XAVIER111: Jake!

MAXIMUS: Whoa! Both the mystery men have broken their silence today!

JAKE_CAN_BREAK17: The final level of Maze Break will be played by us. The Summer Showdown is it. No more Maze Break after that.

JAKE_CAN_BREAK17 is offline

XAVIER111: What?! No way!

MAXIMUS: That's crazy.

AP23 is offline.

I shut down the laptop and quietly slip out Dad's door.

My mind wanders back to the original email from the Maze Break administrators.

'A *once-in-a-lifetime opportunity…*'

'Of course!' I shout in the empty corridor.

It would be mathematically inaccurate to say 'once-in-a-lifetime' if there were going to be more showdowns.

Jake was right.

CHAPTER TEN

Dear Mum, Dad, Max and Louis (can't forget my favourite babysitter!),

The picture on the front of this postcard is the actual ship we're on – it's pretty awesome, although I would've made a few slight changes if I designed it myself (bigger portholes, bigger lifts, bigger waterslide).

I'd also restock the gift shop. I'm going to have a hard time finding you a souvenir in there, Max.

Maybe I should design some souvenirs for them...hang on...that's not such a silly idea.

I'm in design mode now – I'd better start sketching.

Love you, Bella

Phhhwwwwattttt.

'Ew, did you fart, Bella?' Grace asks.

I laugh as I slop sunscreen onto her back. 'No, it was the sunscreen bottle,' I say. 'It must have a lot of air in it.'

I hand the bottle to Emily, who squeezes some onto her hand.

Phhhhwwwwaaaat.

'Pardon me,' Emily laughs.

As Chloe finishes off with the sunscreen, I can't help but notice how different all our skin looks in the sunshine.

'Hey guys,' I say, 'hold out your forearms.'

Emily's arm is pale and freckly. Grace's is fair but with a light tan. Chloe is olive-skinned like her Greek parents and Yiayia. And I'm dark brown like my mum – she was born in India.

'That would make an awesome photo,' I say. 'The contrasting colours of our arms.'

Grace dives into the pool and splashes us all. Her head bobs up and she flicks her hair out of her face.

'What about our hair?' she says. 'That's even more of a contrast, don't you think?'

Emily has long red hair. Grace's is short and blonde. Chloe has black hair in a ponytail. And mine is curly and brown.

'Is something up, Bella?' Chloe asks. 'It's not like you've only just noticed how different-looking we are.'

Emily lowers herself into the pool and swims after Grace. They glide past two Muslim girls in hooded swimsuits with long sleeves that cover their arms and legs.

Emily's wearing a blue tankini. Grace is in

a red racer-back one-piece. Chloe's wearing a purple crop top and black board shorts. I'm in a pink bikini.

'I don't know what it is,' I say. 'Our differences are just standing out a bit more today for some reason.'

Chloe stands up and raises her hands into the shape of a rocket ship. 'Oh well,' she says. 'I guess that can happen sometimes.' She dives in and accidentally splashes so much water into my eyes that I have to blink a few times before I can see properly again.

The Muslim girls start treading water in front of me. They're both clutching identical dolls from the gift shop.

'Look, mine can dive,' says one girl as she dips her doll underwater.

'Mine can float,' says the other as she lays her doll on its back.

It's a shame they can't get dolls that look like them, I think to myself. At least, not on this ship.

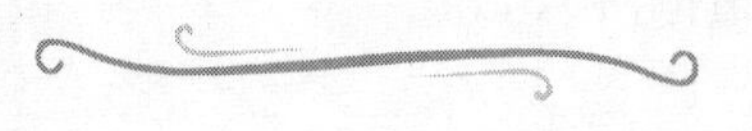

Mission Set Sail: Training regime
30 sit-ups: morning, noon, evening
Jog one lap of main deck: morning, noon, evening
30 bicep curls: morning, noon, evening

'Bicep curls?' Emily asks with a twisted face. 'You want to make me lift weights so I can go in this sailing race with you?'

The other anti-princesses aren't as dedicated to fitness as I am.

'I don't have actual weights,' I say. 'But we can use filled water bottles instead.'

Emily pushes the piece of paper with my workout plan on it back to me.

'Grace, there are only two days until the race,' she says. 'You don't need to be a mathematical genius to realise that's not enough time to gain a significant amount of strength.'

There's no use arguing with Emily when she's made up her mind – and she has a point.

'This is the training regime I've been following,' I say. 'You need to be pretty strong to control the sails, not to mention have good balance to keep the boat steady.'

Emily ignores me as she fires up her laptop.

'Hey, this is important info,' I say. 'Sailing's not a simple sport.'

Emily sighs. 'Grace, you're going to be the skipper,' she says. 'Just order me around as much as you want once we're on the boat.'

Bella and Chloe smile at me from one of the top bunks. They're playing cards, but Emily's willingness to sacrifice the skipper title caught them by surprise.

I'm grateful that I don't have to argue with Emily about who's in charge. I thought I may have had a battle on my hands, since she's used to being the leader and president of the Anti-Princess Club.

But sailing is hard. I've only been learning for four weeks and I'm far from an expert.

I grab a piece of rope from under my bed that I brought along to practise tying knots.

'At least let me show you how to tie a bowline knot,' I say. 'It's what you use to attach the top of the sail to the halyard.'

Emily looks at me blankly.

'Halyard – it's a line used to hoist the sail,' I say.

'Okay,' Emily says, closing her laptop. 'Show me how to tie this knot.'

I take the piece of rope and talk Emily through it.

'Imagine the end of the rope as a rabbit and where

the knot will begin on the standing part as a tree trunk,' I say. 'First, a loop is made near the end of the rope which will be the rabbit's hole. Then the rabbit comes up the hole, goes around the tree from right to left, then back down the hole.'

'There's a rhyme that helps me remember,' Bella calls down from the bunk. 'Up through the rabbit hole, round the big tree, down through the rabbit hole and off goes he.'

I wonder if I should have insisted on Bella pairing up with me for the race.

I think she senses my worry.

'You'll be fine,' Bella says. 'Emily, just listen to Skipper Grace.'

Loggerhead turtle
(Caretta caretta) **facts:**

APPEARANCE:

- The loggerhead turtle gets its name from its large head and thick, strong jaws.
- Fully grown loggerhead turtles are approximately one metre long and can weigh up to 150kg.
- Babies have a dark brown carapace (top of the shell) and a light brown plastron (flat bottom part of the shell).
- Adult shells are heart-shaped and can be light brown, reddish and black.

HABITAT:

- Warm, shallow coastal waters and estuaries.

DIET:

- Shellfish, crabs, sea urchins and jellyfish.

THREATS:

- Land-based predators include birds, goannas, crabs and foxes.
- Sea-based predators include sharks and crocodiles.
- Humans. (Turtles are hunted for their meat, shells and leather in some parts of the world. They're also caught in fishing nets and struck by boats.)
- Pollution.
- Global warming.

I keep the loggerhead turtle fact sheet open on Emily's laptop.

'Come and read this,' I say to the other girls. 'I want you to see how special Cameron is.'

Cameron is what I've named the turtle – I thought Cameron the Caretta had a nice ring to it. It's also one of those names that boys *and* girls have, which works because we don't know if Cameron is a male or female turtle. Although I did flip a coin (not very scientific, I know) to decide if we were going to call Cameron 'he' or 'she' for now – 'she' won.

Grace reads over the fact sheet. 'Wow, that's a lot of threats,' she says.

I nod as I slide off the bed onto the ground alongside Cameron. She's resting in a large tub of sea water that takes up most of the floor space in our cabin. Marnie said she could stay here until we reach Exmouth.

I pour some more water over the towel on top of Cameron's shell. 'The chances of a loggerhead hatchling making it to adulthood are less than one per cent,' I say.

Emily's eyes bulge. When I speak to her in statistics she really gets it. 'What do you think would've happened to her?' she asks.

Cameron opens her eyes for a moment as if she knows we're talking about her. I gently pat the towel.

'She might have been eaten,' I say. 'Or just died of exhaustion.'

'Do you think she's cold?' Bella asks. 'Should we take her out of the water for a while?'

I shake my head. 'It's important to remember that they live in the ocean. That's the best temperature to keep them at.'

Cameron closes her eyes again.

'Let's give her some peace and quiet,' I say. 'And turn the lights off. They like darkness.'

Bella, Grace and Emily head out of the room.

I look back at Cameron before I close the door. 'Just make it to Exmouth,' I whisper. 'It's not far now.'

TO: Ava

FROM: Emily

SUBJECT: Hello from the sea!

Hi sis,

How's life back at home? I hope Mum isn't really making you pop pimples for her. That would be seriously spew-worthy stuff.

It's a shame you couldn't stomach the thought of coming on the cruise with us – it's soooo great.

Dad seems to be having a good time. We've been hanging out a bit, having all our meals together and that sort of thing, but he's also been giving me, Bella, Chloe and Grace lots of time to ourselves.

Oh, how hilarious is this, the other gamers think Dad is me...or that I'm him. I guess an 11-year-old girl didn't fit their image of what a Maze Breaker would look like. I'll let them keep thinking that for now. I've made a mission to reveal my true identity at the showdown – which will make it even better when I win. Talk about pressure, but I'm up for it.

Tomorrow I'm going in a sailing race with Grace. It's a pairs thing, so Grace is going to be the skipper – it's the logical choice because she's been training.

Say hi to Mum for me – tell her I've been wearing heaps of sunscreen.

TTYL,
Emily x

PS Chloe rescued a turtle – and she named it Cameron!

I place my laptop back inside its cover and slide it under a beach towel on my sunlounge.

Just as I'm about to jump in the pool after Bella and Chloe, I spot Grace flapping her arms around in front of Kate, the cruise ship's director of sports.

'Oi, Bella, Chloe!' I call out. 'What's Grace up to?'

They swim up to the pool's edge and lean out on their elbows to get a closer look.

Grace is not only waving her arms, she's stomping her feet too.

'We better go see what's up,' Chloe says. 'They look like they're arguing.'

Chloe and Bella hoist themselves out of the pool. They don't bother drying off as they follow me over to Grace.

'Rules are rules,' Kate is saying to Grace. 'It's for everyone's safety.'

Bella, Chloe and I surround Grace. She's definitely flustered. There are beads of sweat on her forehead, but she hasn't been exercising.

'Emily, apparently you can't be my partner in the regatta,' Grace says. 'There's a rule that there has to be someone aged sixteen or over in every pair.'

I thought Grace must have been having a much more serious argument for her to be so worked up. I can think of a solution to her problem straight away.

'It's no biggie, Grace,' I say. 'I'm sure Dad will take my place.'

Grace grunts and folds her arms.

'Kate asked your dad, but he's never sailed before,' she says. 'So he gave permission for me to be paired with a stranger – if I was okay with it too.'

Kate's gaze shifts to some teenagers crowded around a laptop at a bar on the other side of the deck. I recognise the blue mohawk on one of them straight away – Maximus.

'Is it Maximus?' I ask.

'No, it's Anthony.' Kate points at another guy in the group wearing a Maze Break T-shirt.

'AKA Ant16. He's sailed before.'

I size up Ant16. I'm secretly pleased that I'm only one place behind him on the Maze Break leaderboard. I wonder how he'd react if he knew an eleven-year-old was hot on his heels.

'Can't you just pair him with someone else?' I ask Kate. 'And let Grace choose a different partner?'

Kate looks at her watch. She's getting impatient. 'I'm sorry, but all our dinghies have been claimed,' she says. 'Grace, you're free to pull out of the regatta if you're that upset.'

Grace's lips twist into a cat's-bottom pucker.

'You wouldn't seriously pull out, would you?' Chloe asks.

I'm ready to support whatever Grace decides…until it dawns on me.

'You have to go in it!' I yell. 'You can't forget Mission Set Sail: Team Anti-Princess win the mini-regatta. The anti-princesses have never left a mission incomplete!'

Kate tries to hide a chuckle behind her clipboard.

'If you like, I can insist Anthony keeps your name,' she says. 'Team Anti-Princess.'

Grace groans as she gives the teenage gamers another once-over.

'Fine,' she says. 'I'll race with him.'

Chloe crosses one leg over the other and wriggles as though she's doing some sort of clumsy dance move.

'Can you just stay still a little longer?' I ask. 'I'm nearly done.'

Chloe's cheeks puff up with air as she holds her breath.

Pfffffffffft.

The air escapes through her mouth in a long fart sound. Chloe uncrosses her legs. 'Sorry, Bella!' she yells, running for the bathroom. 'I can't hold on any longer.'

I hold up my sketchpad and look at what I've created so far.

'Give us a look,' Grace says.

I flip the page around to face Grace and Emily. They're sitting on the floor with Cameron.

'That looks just like her,' Emily says. 'You're so talented, Bella.'

I'm pretty pleased with my sketch of Chloe. I've got the shape of her glasses just right, and the proportions of her body are spot on – medium height, shorter legs than Grace, but longer than Emily's and mine. She's wearing her favourite outfit – a lab coat over a skirt and top.

Shhhhhhhhh.

The toilet flushes and Chloe emerges looking relieved.

'That's better,' she says. 'Now, how was I standing?'

'You can sit down now,' I say, tapping the bed next to me. 'I've finished drawing my Chloe doll.'

Chloe flops down on the bed. 'Hey, that does look like me,' she says. 'But what do you mean by "doll"?'

I flick to the next page where I've started sketching Emily. 'I'm designing some dolls,' I say. 'You know, like toys.'

Emily sticks out her tongue. 'That's a bit spew-worthy, isn't it? I didn't think dolls were your thing, Bella. What happened to designing buildings or another billycart or planetarium?'

I look at the real-life Emily's freckles on her nose and copy them onto my drawing of her.

'Maybe I would've been more into playing with dolls when I was little if there were some in the shops that looked like us,' I say. 'You know, with different-coloured skin, and hair and clothes like we wear.'

Grace swaps places with Chloe and starts doing some tricep dips on the edge of the bed.

'And maybe I would've been more into playing with dolls if they actually did things,' she says. 'Like bend and twist.'

Grace is onto something. I make a note.

Grace doll: Bendable limbs

Chloe pats Cameron's shell. 'And maybe

I would've been more into dolls if they came with interesting accessories…not just fake little plastic bits and pieces, but things that actually work.'

Chloe doll: Comes with real magnifying glass

Emily pauses. I wonder if anything would make her want to play with dolls.

'Maybe I would've wanted a doll if it actually said something,' she says. 'And not just anything …something useful or interesting.'

I make another note.

Emily doll: Talks, recites mathematical rules

'What about you, Bella?' Grace asks between dips. 'What would've made you more interested in a doll – other than having one that looked like a real girl?'

A doll's house seems like the logical answer for me, but Mum and Dad gave me one when I was four and I was never really interested in it. I think it was just too ordinary for a budding architect.

I run my hand along the cabin wall. 'Maybe a house,' I say. 'But a unique house.'

Bella doll: With custom-made houseboat

'Don't close your sketchpad yet,' Emily says. 'Don't you want to set a mission to get these toys happening?'

I make a final note.

Mission Toy: Get Emily, Bella, Grace and and Chloe made into dolls

'All in favour?' I ask.

Everyone raises their hands.

'Let's knock those boring things off the shelves,' I say.

It looks like someone took a pile of gigantic white napkins and threw them into the sea. But it's really just the floating sails of capsized dinghies.

Two boats at a time have been racing around a course marked with buoys. Not many are managing to actually cross the finish line, but the ones who do have their times recorded. The fastest time wins the regatta.

'No one seems to be very experienced,' I say. 'Some people can't even tell the difference between windward and leeward.'

Anthony bites his lip.

'You do know the difference between windward and leeward, don't you?' I ask.

'Windward is the direction from where the wind is blowing, leeward is downwind. That first buoy is the windward mark because it's just upwind from the start and finish line. The second buoy is the leeward mark because it's downwind. We go around both in an anti-clockwise direction before we cross the finish line.'

Anthony yawns and refuses to make eye contact.

'Look, you can be the skipper,' he says. 'But that doesn't mean you can talk to me like I'm a baby. I know how to sail, okay?'

I'm not convinced. But I figure it's best not to start a fight with someone I'm about to be alone with on the water.

I clip my lifejacket up as Anthony heaves our dinghy into the water.

'Can I double-check the rigging before we launch?' I ask.

Anthony makes a *pffffft* sound. 'I've checked everything. Let's just get to the start line before we're too late.'

I wave to Emily, Bella, Chloe and Mr Martin. They're sitting on the sand with a sign:

GO TEAM ANTI-PRINCESS!

I raise the mainsail and grab the tiller to guide us to the start line in the water. We're in the last race of the day.

'Aren't you going to hoist the jib, Anthony?' I ask.

He stares at me blankly.

'The jib – the front sail,' I say.

My heart starts to pound a little faster as I check my lifejacket buckle is fastened properly.

Anthony fumbles around with the sheets and eventually gets the jib up.

He looks back at me proudly. 'See, I know what I'm doing,' he says. 'I'm a little out of practice, but it's coming back.'

Another dinghy with what looks like a

mother and daughter team is waiting to race us. A speedboat with *Capricorn Princess* crewmembers onboard is also at the start line, and there are four lifeguards on jetskis patrolling the course.

Kate, the ship's sports director, calls out from a megaphone on the speedboat.

'Before I sound the horn, I just want to emphasise that safety comes first!' she says. 'If you capsize, don't be embarrassed – we'll send a jetski over straight away and pull your dinghy back to shore if need be.'

Anthony's Adam's apple momentarily bulges. I think he's scared.

'On your marks!' Kate calls out. 'Get set!'

Hooooonnnnnnnnnnk.

Our dinghy slowly edges away from the mother and daughter team as their mainsail luffs and they figure out how to tighten it.

'Amateurs!' Anthony calls out.

If I wasn't too busy concentrating on steering, I'd lecture Anthony on bad sportsmanship.

We're running with the wind behind our backs, which isn't the best case scenario, but I know how to go faster.

'Pull the jib in tight, Anthony!' I yell. 'The wind will fill it.'

He does what I say and the dinghy sails faster, straight towards the windward mark.

I move the tiller to steer us around the buoy.

'Good work, Anthony!' I call out. 'But we have to jibe now!'

He turns to me and bites his lip again. That must be his way of admitting he doesn't understand.

'Jibe!' I yell. 'We need to put the stern through the eye of the wind! Watch out for the boom as I pull the main sail across!'

Anthony bites his lip again.

'The boom!' I yell. 'It's the horizontal pole attached to the mast!'

Anthony nods as if a light bulb has just turned on in his brain.

'Jibing now!' I yell.

The boom only just misses the top of his head as it swings across the boat.

'Good work!' I yell.

I spot the other dinghy out of the corner of my eye. They're just turning around the first buoy as we make our way around the second.

'Almost there!' I yell.

My eyes are focused on the finish line about twenty metres ahead, but Anthony suddenly looks back and up.

'Oh no,' he says.

I tilt my head up to the sky just as the mainsail flops off the mast and into the middle of the boat.

The weight of it sends the boat toppling over with Anthony and me inside it.

I swallow a mouthful of sea water, but my lifejacket brings me bobbing back to the surface.

Cough, cough, cough. Cough. Cough.

Anthony is spluttering next to me.

'You should've let me check the rigging!' I yell.

'The sail mustn't have been tied up properly!'

Anthony grabs the hull and wipes some water from his eyes.

'I tied it myself,' he says. 'I tied a perfect reef knot.'

I slap myself in the forehead. 'You don't use reef knots to tie the head of a sail to halyards! They always slip! Everyone knows you use a bowline knot for that!'

Anthony's lips quiver. I think he might cry.

A jetski pulls up next to our capsized dinghy.

'Climb on,' says the lifeguard. 'You don't have to finish the race.'

I squint back at the last buoy and see the other dinghy struggling to turn around it.

I look the other way towards the finish line. It's less than fifteen metres away.

Emily's words from the cruise ship ring through my head: *The anti-princesses have never left a mission incomplete!*

'We have to finish,' I say. 'I'm not getting on that jetski.'

Anthony scoffs. 'It will take us forever just to get the boat upright again and the sails hoisted.'

He's right. We're so close that re-launching would be a waste of time. 'Let's just swim,' I say. 'We'll push the boat over the line.'

I don't wait for Anthony to answer. I use all the strength I can muster to push against the hull while kicking my legs.

Anthony copies. It's a lot easier with two sets of arms and legs. 'Push!' I yell.

'Can you still order me around when we're not in the boat?' Anthony asks.

'I'm still the skipper until the race is over,' I say.

Hooooooooonk.

The sound of the horn signals the first team crossing the line. It's not us.

The mother and daughter team beat us by a split second. I lean my forehead against the hull to catch my breath.

Kate's voice comes over the megaphone from her speedboat. 'Well, it wasn't the most conventional finish,' she says. 'But we've just had the fastest time recorded of all the races. Team Girl Power wins the regatta – Team Anti-Princess places second.'

The other team sails over to our capsized dinghy.

'Congratulations,' I say. 'It must have been awesome to race with someone from your own family.'

The woman laughs. 'We're not related,' she says. 'We only just met. We got paired together by the cruise ship staff.'

The girl laughs too. 'I can't believe we won,' she says. 'It's all about trusting your partner.'

I can hear Emily, Bella and Chloe cheering from the sand.

I suddenly realise even the best athletes in the world don't get to pick their teammates.

Kate throws two red and white-striped life rings into the water from the speedboat.

'It's okay, I'll swim to the boat!' I call out. 'I don't need rescuing!'

I step onto a mini ladder hanging over the edge of the boat and climb up.

'Sometimes you win, sometimes you lose,' Kate says.

I shake my head. 'Sometimes you win, sometimes you learn.'

Mission Set Sail: incomplete.

I stroke Cameron's eyelids. They flutter a little, but she doesn't open them. 'I think we got here just in time,' I say. 'She seems weaker.'

Marnie has driven me, Mr Martin and the anti-princesses to the veterinary clinic after Grace's regatta.

We decided we would rather be with Cameron than join the rest of the cruise ship passengers snorkelling.

'You're a very selfless bunch missing out on Ningaloo,' Marnie says. 'And you've done a great job keeping the turtle comfortable for this long, Chloe.'

A woman with a stethoscope around her neck meets us in the foyer.

'I'm Sharna Meyer,' she says. 'I hear you have a sick turtle.'

I pull the wet towels off Cameron's back so Dr Meyer has a proper view.

'You've done the right thing keeping it in a few inches of sea water,' she says. 'Let's take it into my clinic for an examination.'

Marnie and Mr Martin each grab a handle on the tub. We follow Dr Meyer to a brightly lit room that smells like a mixture of cleaning products and sea salt.

Dr Meyer lifts Cameron out of the tub and places her on a table in the middle of the room.

I hold my breath nervously as she feels Cameron's neck then shines a small torch onto her closed eyelids.

'It's alive,' Dr Meyer says.

Phew.

I feel a tear slip out of the corner of my right eye.

'What do you think it is, doctor?' Mr Martin asks.

Dr Meyer gently flips Cameron onto her back and runs her fingers along her plastron. She places Cameron the right way up and gives her shell a pat.

'I can't be sure, but I wouldn't be surprised if it's ingested a foreign object,' Dr Meyer says. 'It's very common in the turtles we see here, but I'll need to take an X-ray to confirm my suspicions.'

I spy an X-ray machine in the corner of the room.

'I'm afraid you'll have to leave the room while I do the X-ray,' she says. 'We don't like to risk unnecessary exposure to radiation.'

My bottom lip juts out. I wish I could stay, but I've read about the dangers of radiation exposure.

'It will only take a few minutes,' Dr Meyer says.

Emily lightly pushes me towards the door.

'Be brave, Cameron,' I say.

Everyone except me takes a seat in the foyer.

I pace backwards and forwards, staring at the floor.

'I bet it's a plastic bag,' I say. 'People just throw them away and they end up in the ocean. The poor turtles and fish mistake them for jellyfish.'

Bella paces with me. 'That's terrible, Chloe,' she says. 'Maybe I'll design some sort of filter for drains that catches rubbish before it pours into the sea.'

Back and forth. Back. Forth. Back. Forth.

We pace for what seems like hours, but is merely minutes.

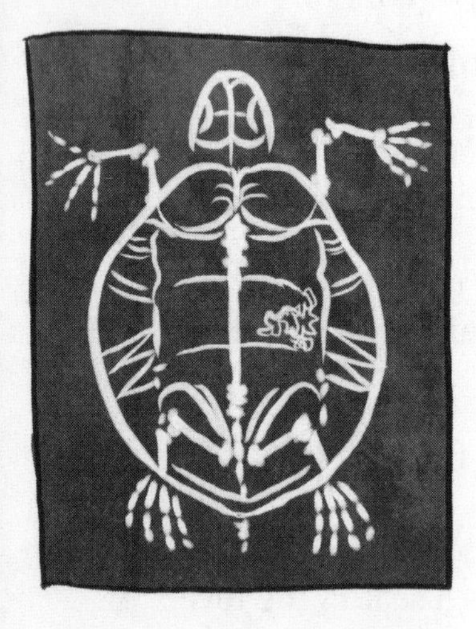

Dr Meyer reappears in the foyer.

'I found the problem,' she says. 'Come in and I'll show you.'

Dr Meyer turns on a monitor mounted on the wall and a black and white image of Cameron's insides appears.

Dr Meyer points to a greyish blob on the screen. 'That's it there, in the stomach,' she says. 'Latex.'

I squint at the blurry spot behind Dr Meyer's fingertip. 'It seems so small,' I say.

Mr Martin puts his hand up as if he's in a classroom and Dr Meyer is the teacher. 'If it's that small, shouldn't Cameron be able to poo it out?' he asks.

'Balloons usually get stuck in the throat or intestinal tract,' Dr Meyer says. 'Sadly, I don't hold much hope.'

A balloon. Of course.

'How do you know it's a balloon?' Bella asks.

'Turtles swallow them all the time,' Dr Meyer says. 'They really are one of the worst hazards for marine life. People let the balloons float into the sky at celebrations and they often end up in the ocean.'

Even in the X-ray the balloon looks like a tiny squid. Cameron must have mistaken it for a snack.

'Will you be able to get it out?' I ask.

Dr Meyer shakes her head as she switches the monitor off. 'We can't perform surgery like that on turtles. Cutting through the shell is too risky...and Cameron is already very sick.'

My eyes sting with tears. I start to sniffle as I walk towards Cameron. I stroke her head. 'Can you hear me, Cameron?' I whisper. 'I just want you to know how brave you've been.'

Emily, Grace and Bella surround me.

'I've always wanted to see a *Caretta caretta*,' I say. 'I thought I might see one out snorkelling, but this has been even better. I got to care for you. I even got to name you.'

I bend down and kiss Cameron's head. 'I hope you pull through,' I say. 'Whatever happens, I'll miss you.'

I feel the anti-princesses' hands on my back. 'We all will.'

At least 96.8 per cent of the *Capricorn Princess's* passengers are talking about the snorkelling at Ningaloo Reef yesterday.

Which makes it 127 times more difficult to deal with the sadness we're all feeling after saying goodbye to Cameron.

Dad is sleeping it off in his suite. Grace is swimming laps. Chloe has her head in an astronomy journal. And Bella is sketching another one of her dolls – I think it's the one modelled on herself.

'I'm going to move away from the pool a bit,' I say to Chloe and Bella. 'I don't want my laptop to get splashed.'

They barely look up as I grab my computer and look for a spot to practise Maze Break.

I see an empty table with two chairs fifteen metres away from the edge of the pool. A meteor would have to land in the water for any droplets to hit me from that far away.

I take a seat and log into the Maze Break website. I leave the chat function off but notice Jake_can_break17, Skywalker2000 and Will_will_will are online.

I start to move my pigeon avatar through the next maze. In the earlier levels, the mazes were much easier and you could simply turn left at every junction and backtrack to eventually find your way out. Now, some of the mazes are disjointed and sometimes you get plonked in the middle of one to find your way out instead of starting at an entrance.

'If only there was an algorithm you could use for them all,' I mutter.

A deep voice replies from behind me. 'There is.'

I pause my game and crane my neck around. There's a guy, sitting with his back to me, at the table next to mine. He's wearing a pale blue rugby-style top with JW on the back.

I lean sideways and notice he's playing a computer too. 'What did you say?' I ask.

He doesn't turn around. 'I said, there is an algorithm. It's called Trémaux's Algorithm. Trémaux was a French mathematician, and his basic rule for getting through any maze was: when you get to a junction you haven't already visited, take any path. When you get to a dead end, turn around and go back. When you get to a junction that you have already visited, take a path that you haven't previously taken. If you've already taken each path, then take the one that you haven't taken more than once. If you've taken all the paths more than once, turn back to the last junction you visited.'

I process what he's saying. 'So, basically, as long as you don't take the same path more than twice you should find your way out,' I say.

'I'm pretty sure I already follow that rule, even though I didn't know it was invented by someone called Trémaux.'

The JW on his back jiggles around a bit as he laughs. 'Well, you're a natural-born mathematician,' he says. 'You must be in the Maze Break showdown.'

I gulp. JW is onto me. 'Um,' I say. 'You just reminded me, I need to go and find my dad.'

I shut my laptop and slide it under my arm. I have to get away before JW ruins my entire mission.

'Your dad?' he asks. I stand up and he turns around. He has braces and a fluffy blond moustache. I'd guess he's about seventeen.

'Well, your dad must be very smart too,' he says. 'I look forward to competing against him.'

I keep my head down and shuffle back towards Bella, Chloe and Grace.

I can't believe I almost got caught out.

I grab a roll of toilet paper from the shelf and examine the tiny ships printed on each square of tissue.

The shop assistant comes out from behind the gift shop counter and nods at the roll in my hands.

'That's printed with illustrations of the *Capricorn Princess*,' he says. 'So you can remember your cruise every time you go to the bathroom at home.'

I put my hand over my mouth to cover my laughter. The other anti-princesses aren't so discreet.

'Wow,' Grace laughs. 'I don't like princesses, but I'm not sure I'd wipe my bum with one.'

The shop assistant folds his arms across his chest. He's not smiling.

'Sorry,' I say. 'It's an inside joke, nothing personal.'

Emily takes a snow globe from a shelf and shakes it up. Tiny white pieces of plastic rain down on a polar bear under a palm tree.

'Correct me if I'm wrong,' she laughs. 'But the Capricorn Princess doesn't cruise into the Arctic Circle – does it?'

Bahahahahahaha.

Chloe lets out a deep belly laugh – the first since she said goodbye to Cameron. 'No, I don't believe we will be entering the habitat of any polar bears. Although I'm pretty sure palm trees don't grow in the Arctic Circle, so maybe the polar bear is lost…and it brought the snow to Western Australia.'

I take the snow globe and slide it back in its place. 'Shhhh. I don't want to upset the shop assistant too much before I ask to see the manager.'

Emily, Chloe and Grace straighten themselves up and stop laughing.

'That's better,' I say. 'Now, back me up here.'

I clear my throat. The shop assistant is counting coins. His name badge says *Doug*.

'Hello, Doug,' I say.

He puts the last of the coins into the cash register and closes the drawer with a *ping*.

'Didn't want to take the toilet paper?' he asks.

I smile politely. 'Maybe next time,' I say. 'May I speak to the manager? You see, I'm a designer, and I've created a product that I think would sell wonderfully in a gift shop.'

Doug smirks. 'I'm the shop manager,' he says. 'So I'm your best bet for any sales pitches.'

Three women in sparkly kaftans line up behind me with three of the gift shop's dolls, some rolls of toilet paper, a stuffed turtle toy and two snow globes.

'Excuse me while I serve these lovely ladies,' Doug says.

I step aside and try to bite my tongue as Doug puts the first doll into a paper bag, but I can't stop myself.

'Who are those dolls for?' I ask.

The woman in the sparkliest gold kaftan answers. 'They're for our granddaughters,' she says. 'They love dolls.'

Doug scans the second doll.

'Did you think it was a bit strange that all the dolls looked the same?' I ask. 'With their blonde hair and blue eyes, and the exact same outfit?'

Doug frowns at me. He must be afraid I'm trying to do him out of a sale, but I'm just trying to prove that kids would like a choice of dolls.

I pull my sketchpad out of my bag and flip it open to my drawing of Emily.

'I'm a designer and I've designed a range of

dolls that look like real girls,' I say. 'Starting with me and my three best friends.'

The woman pulls a pair of glasses from a chain around her neck onto her nose. She takes my pad and peers at the drawing closely, then she looks up at Emily.

'This really does look like you,' she says. 'What lovely red hair you have.'

Emily groans quietly. She hates it when people compliment her on how she looks. Mainly because they focus on her hair and freckles before anything else – like her interests or awesome talents.

'Not only does the doll look like a real girl,' I say, 'but it does cool things too. This one, for example, can tell you how many bits are in a byte.'

It's Doug's turn to laugh now.

'I don't think girls are interested in computers,' he says. 'They just want something pretty, like the dolls we sell.'

The woman takes off her glasses and hands Doug a fifty-dollar note.

'I think you're wrong there, sir,' she says. 'My granddaughter loves dolls and knows how to read binary code – she's even teaching me.'

The woman takes her bag of souvenirs. 'Good luck with your dolls,' she says. 'I'd buy one.'

The sparkly kaftans disappear out the door as another three women walk in and head straight towards the display of the cruise ship's dolls.

'Can I show you my other designs, Doug?' I ask. 'Do you think the ship would be interested in stocking them?'

Doug yawns. 'There's nothing I can do for you,' he says. 'The dolls we stock are made by a big toy manufacturing company. And, as you can see, they're flying off the shelves.'

I madly flick to my sketch of the Chloe doll and hold it up. 'But if people had something like this as an option, you might be surprised what actually sells,' I say. 'This doll has its own magnifying glass.'

Doug nods his head towards the exit.

'I can't help you,' he says. 'You don't even have a product. All you have is sketches.'

Grace puts her hands on my shoulders and pulls me away from the counter. 'Let's leave it for now,' she whispers.

I turn away from Doug in a huff. 'He'll see. The anti-princess dolls will be huge, and he'll be kicking himself.'

Dear Mum, Dad, Tom, Oliver and Harry,

This postcard will probably arrive home after I do, but I thought it would make a good little memory of the trip.

I came second in the regatta! Those lessons really paid off – thanks again, I know they must have been expensive.

I was the skipper and I had to race with a 16-year-old named Anthony. He was a royal pain. He made out like he was an experienced sailor, but he didn't even know what a jib was!

I've had an awesome time and haven't felt cooped up. But I'm looking forward to going for a run on real land very soon.

Miss you all,

Love, Grace

'Hey, Grace!' a voice calls out from across the deck. Anthony is waving at me.

'What does he want?' Chloe asks.

Anthony throws a beach towel around his shoulders and walks over to the sunlounges where the anti-princesses and I are writing postcards – all of us except Bella, who's still sketching dolls.

'Don't forget he's a Maze Breaker,' Emily hisses. 'We can't blow my cover.'

Anthony leans against the back of Bella's sunlounge and sneaks a peek at her sketchpad. 'Cool drawing,' he says. 'Looks like you, Grace.'

Bella turns the page so I can see it.

'Yep, that's me,' I say. 'Or me as a doll, anyway.'

Anthony looks at Bella's sketch again. 'That's interesting,' he says. 'And a bit of a coincidence. My parents sell dolls for a living – well, not just dolls, but all sorts of stuff.'

Emily and Bella try to speak at once, but Emily's voice dominates. 'Do they sell video games?' she asks.

'I wish,' Anthony says. 'Are you a gamer too? I heard your dad is – he's AP23, right?'

Emily looks down and pretends to keep writing on her postcard.

Bella seizes upon the silence.

'Are your parents on the cruise?' she asks. 'Do you reckon they'd take a look at my drawings?'

Anthony shifts from one foot to the other. 'Um, look, that's not really why I came over,' he says. 'Grace, I just wanted to say sorry for being a bit of a dud in the regatta.'

The truth is, I got over the knot drama the second we crossed the finish line. But to keep him here for Bella's sake, I pretend I'm still cranky.

'Yeah, well, it was pretty silly,' I say. 'Any experienced sailor knows you always use a bowline knot to attach a sail like that.'

Anthony turns to leave.

'You know, we could've had a serious accident,' I say. 'Or drowned.'

Anthony frowns. 'That's a bit dramatic, isn't it?' he says. 'I told you I'm sorry. What more do you want?'

I look sideways at Bella while trying to keep up the act. 'There is a way you could make it up to me,' I say.

Anthony sighs. 'And what would that be?'

I reach across to Bella's lap and take her sketchpad. 'Show your parents Bella's sketches,' I say. 'They're dolls modelled on us – real girls – and we think they should stock them in the *Capricorn Princess* gift shop… and in toy shops across the world.'

Anthony sighs again. 'Okay,' he says. 'I'll show Mum and Dad your drawings. I'm heading back to our suite now.'

I call after him. 'You forgot to call me skipper!'

Anthony glances back and we both laugh.

Bella jumps up and gives me a hug. 'Do you think they'll like them?' she asks.

I put my arm around her shoulders.

'If they don't, we'll throw them all overboard,' I say. 'Anthony's experienced at falling into the water.'

Attention guests. To celebrate the last night aboard the Capricorn Princess, *our crew are throwing an impromptu party on the main deck near the waterslide in five minutes. All welcome. See you there.*

The voice on the loudspeaker is drowned out by a cheesy pop song.

Good times, baby, yeah! Everybody celebrate! Wooooh!

'Somebody make it stop,' I say, burying my head under the pillow on my bed.

Bella moans from the bottom bunk across from mine: 'Now.'

Emily hangs her head over the side of the bunk above mine.

'I'm sorry, everyone,' she says. 'It hasn't been the best few days, has it? I feel like it's all my fault because I brought you on the cruise.'

I remove the pillow and sit up so I'm face-to-Emily's-upside-down-face.

'Don't be silly,' I say. 'I'm really happy we came – we've had a great time, and your Maze Break showdown is yet to come. I'm just feeling sorry for myself about Cameron.'

Bella sits up and swings her legs around so her feet hit the floor. 'And I'm just grumpy about the gift shop manager not taking me seriously,' she says. 'It's not your fault, Emily.'

Grace jumps down from her bunk and squeezes in bed next to me. 'Maybe that party will be the best thing for all of us,' she says. 'Something to cheer everyone up.'

Knock, knock, knock. Knock. Knock.

'Come in!' Emily calls. Mr Martin pops his head in. He's wearing a party hat.

'Well?' he says. 'Are you girls ready to party? Everybody celebrate! Wooooh!'

I can't help but grin at Mr Martin's dorkiness. It's something my own baba would do, or Yiayia.

'Where did you get that hat?' Emily asks as we all head into the corridor.

'I was on the deck when they were setting up,' Mr Martin says. 'You should see it up there – it's very festive.'

We climb the steps – at Grace's insistence – until we reach the main deck.

'See what I mean?' Mr Martin says.

Everyone around us is laughing and dancing, but all I see is red – in more ways than one.

'Nooooooooooooo!' I scream.

A few heads turn to stare at me, but the music is too loud for most people to hear.

'What is it, Chloe?' Mr Martin asks.

I point at the tables, the chairs, the bars, the sunlounges, the railings. 'They're everywhere!' I scream. 'Everywhere!'

Grace frantically spins in a circle.

'What should we do?' Bella asks.

'There are hundreds,' Emily says.

Mr Martin still hasn't figured out the cause of our stress. 'What's wrong, girls?' he asks.

Emily unties the nearest piece of string and pulls the bright red globe down to her dad's eye level. 'Balloons, Dad!' she yells. 'They're all over the boat!'

I scramble towards the closest table and take an umbrella out of an empty cocktail glass. I use the pointy toothpick stem to start bursting balloons.

Pop, pop, pop. Pop. Pop. Pop.

Emily, Grace and Bella do the same. Even Mr Martin joins in.

Everybody celebr—

The music comes to a halt. I don't care. I just keep popping and carefully placing the burst pieces of latex into my pockets.

Pop, pop, pop. Pop. Pop. Pop.

Now everyone is staring at us.

'What's going on here?' Two crew members rush over. One of them grabs me by the wrist mid-pop.

'These balloons can't be here,' I say. 'They're turtle killers. You can't have this many balloons in the middle of the ocean, right in the middle of their habitat!'

Marnie runs over to the woman holding my wrist.

'It's okay, Karen,' she says. 'Let her go. I know her.'

Karen releases my wrist and steps away.

'Chloe, I understand why you're upset,' Marnie says. 'Just leave the balloons for now.

When the party wraps up, I'll help you pop them all, okay?'

I put my umbrella toothpick in my pocket.

'You can make sure none end up in the water,' Marnie says.

I grab the back of a chair with both hands and take a deep breath to calm down. 'Okay, but that's not the end of it,' I say. I turn to Emily. 'Can I propose a mission?'

Emily takes her notepad out of her pocket. 'Go ahead,' she says.

'Mission Cameron: Ban balloons from the *Capricorn Princess*,' I say.

Emily writes the mission down. 'All in favour?'

The anti-princesses raise their hands. Mr Martin and Marnie do too.

A *Capricorn Princess* crewmember with a clipboard under his arm is waiting outside the door to our suite. His name tag says *Buddy*.

'AP23?' he asks in the direction of Bella, Grace, Chloe and me.

I point to Dad. 'Ah, um,' I say. 'Meet my dad.'

Buddy frowns as he refers to his clipboard.

'That's odd,' he says. 'I have AP23 written down here as being Emily Martin, who I assumed was a girl.'

The anti-princesses freeze.

'How does he know AP23's real name?' I whisper to Dad.

Dad scratches his chin. 'He must have our proper details from when I made the booking,' he says. 'I didn't know about the big charade back then.'

Buddy narrows his eyes. 'Big charade?'

I survey the corridor. There's no one else within earshot, so I figure it's best to come clean.

'I'm AP23,' I say. 'But since we got here, everyone has just assumed my dad is the Maze Breaker.'

Buddy chuckles. 'That's understandable,' he says. 'You are the only female player. And you're definitely the youngest.'

I open our cabin door and grab my lanyard from the inside handle.

'See this?' I say. 'I'm the president of a club – the Anti-Princess Club – and I set this mission with the other club members on the first day of the cruise.'

Buddy reads my scrawl.

Mission Maze Break: Reveal the real AP23 at the Top Ten Summer Showdown – and win.

'So, the thing is, Buddy,' I say, 'I don't need rescuing, but if there's anything you can do to help me achieve that mission, I'd be very grateful.'

Buddy pulls a piece of paper from his clipboard and hands it to me.

'It's the rules for the Maze Break Showdown,' he says. 'That's why I'm here – to give you the rules. I think you'll find that it doesn't say anything about not being able to take a supporter into the gaming room with you. If you and your dad go in together, everyone will still think he's AP23 and you're just there for luck.'

I skim over the rules.

1. Maze Breakers to arrive in gaming room on level six at 1:30pm.
2. Maze Breakers will be seated in gaming booths scattered throughout the room.
3. Maze Breakers will be given the same maze to break, with the countdown beginning at 2pm.
4. Upon exiting the maze, Maze Breakers will be given a mathematical problem to solve.
5. The first Maze Breaker to solve the problem wins the showdown.

'Thanks, Buddy,' I say. 'That's a big help.'

He holds his hand out for a high-five.

'Don't mention it,' he says. 'But pretending to be someone else isn't the most important part of the mission you've got written down there.'

I hit his hand.

'You've actually got to win the thing,' he continues. 'No one can help you do that.'

I hold my finger out and trace imaginary lines between the stars.

'I just discovered a new constellation,' I say. 'If you join that really bright one to the left with that one to the south and then that one in the east, you get a giant bum.'

Emily, Grace and Chloe laugh.

'You're a crack-up, Bella,' Grace says. 'Get it? Crack-up – bum crack?'

I laugh so much I almost choke on my hot chocolate.

'This is an astronomer's dream,' Chloe says. 'There's no light pollution out here like there is on land. We could spot sky butts all night.'

Mr Martin let us bring some blankets up to

the deck so we could celebrate our last night on the cruise in our own way.

A bunch of other families must have had the same idea, because there are little huddles of people dotted all around us.

'There they are.'

Mr Martin's voice makes us all turn around.

He's standing a few metres away with Anthony and another man and woman. The woman is holding a sketchpad.

I wipe some hot chocolate off my chin.

'You must be Bella Singh,' the woman says. 'Your name is on the inside cover of this pad.'

I stand up and shake her hand. 'That's me,' I say. 'And these are my friends, Emily Martin, Grace Bennett and Chloe Karalis.'

'I'm Jacklyn Murphy, and this is my husband Warren,' the woman says. 'And you've met our son Anthony – or Ant, as we like to call him.'

Mr Martin drags three chairs over for the Murphys to sit down.

Jacklyn opens my sketchpad to the illustration of Emily. 'And Ant showed us your doll drawings,' she says. 'I love them all.'

She points to the notes written next to Emily. 'It says here that this doll will be able to recite mathematical rules,' Jacklyn says. 'What do you mean?'

'Like there are eight bits in a byte,' Emily says. 'The Emily doll will teach kids to read binary code.'

Jacklyn nods with approval. 'Well, I think it's a wonderful idea to blend education with play,' she says. 'I could've done with something like this when I was a child.'

She turns to the next page – my drawing of Chloe.

'And this one has glasses, like your friend,' Jacklyn says, nodding towards Chloe.

'It actually is Chloe,' I say. 'I got the idea when I saw the blonde dolls in the gift store here on the cruise ship. They all looked the same, and I just thought it would be awesome for kids to be able to play with dolls that actually looked like real people.'

Warren wriggles in his seat. He seems a little uncomfortable. 'You don't like the dolls in the gift shop?' he asks. 'The ones with the leis and the grass skirts?'

I poke my tongue out and go cross-eyed to be funny. 'Urgh, no,' I say. 'Those dolls are what we call "spew-worthy".'

Jacklyn fans her face with my sketchpad as if she's flustered. 'We distribute those dolls,' she says. 'They sell well, but I guess we don't really offer people much choice.'

Anthony sniggers behind his mum's back.

'I'm sorry, Mrs Murphy,' I say. 'I didn't mean to offend you.'

Jacklyn reaches into her handbag and pulls out a business card. 'No offence taken,' she says. 'You've inspired us, Bella. We'd like to order some prototypes based on these sketches of yours. Would you give us permission to send them to one of the manufacturers we deal with?'

I jump up and down, then throw my arms around her neck. 'That would be awesome!' I say.

Mission Toy: complete.

'Oh, but one more thing,' I say.

Jacklyn straightens her top. I think she was taken aback by the hug. 'Yes?'

'If you like the prototypes, and the dolls are manufactured in bulk, can you make sure they're stocked here on the *Capricorn Princess*?' I ask.

Jacklyn looks at Warren and he shrugs.

'Why not?' she says. 'Let's throw a scientist, a mathematician, an athlete and an artist among the girls in the grass skirts.'

Chapter Twenty-Three

Grace

I bend into a downward dog pose as quietly as I can. It's hard enough trying to do my morning yoga in this tiny cabin without having to worry about waking up the other anti-princesses.

Knock, knock, knock.

'What the?' Emily jolts awake. I try not to laugh at the drool running down her chin.

'Too early,' Bella moans. Chloe rolls towards the wall, pretending she didn't hear a thing.

I put my ear against the door. 'Who is it?' I ask.

A voice softly answers: 'It's me, Marnie.'

I twist the lock and let her in. 'Sorry it's so early,' she says. 'But I have a surprise for you all – if you're up for it.'

The anti-princesses are intrigued enough to open their eyes. 'What is it?' I ask.

Marnie pulls a hand from behind her back and dangles a snorkelling mask in front of me. 'We cruise into our home port this evening,' she says. 'But, right now, we're anchored near an awesome reef. It's no Ningaloo, but I wanted you to get some snorkelling in before the end of the trip.'

Knock, knock, knock. Knock. Knock.

Mr Martin pokes his head around the door. 'Hurry up,' he says. 'The fish are waiting.'

Marnie ducks back into the corridor as Emily, Bella and Chloe jump out of bed and we all start rummaging through our suitcases for swimsuits.

I'm still wriggling into mine as we sprint up the steps to the main deck.

'Kate, the sports director, has a tender waiting for us over here,' Marnie says. 'It's what we use to get passengers on and off the ship while we're still at sea.'

Kate hands us lifejackets before we all climb into an inflatable boat attached to the side of the ship.

'Ready to go!' she calls out, as the boat is slowly lowered into the water.

The hull hits the ocean's surface as Marnie starts the engine and grabs the tiller.

'Get your masks and flippers on,' she says. 'It's just a little way over here.'

Chloe squeezes my hand.

'I'm a bit scared,' she whispers. 'This is the middle of the ocean – we might not be the top of the food chain around here, if you get what I mean.'

I look back at the *Capricorn Princess* as the tender comes to a stop. We're not far away. Surely there's someone up there looking out for us.

'I'll stay in this boat keeping a close eye on you,' Kate says. 'Marnie will be in the water with you. Stay close together and you'll be fine. The reef has a diameter of about a hundred metres. If you get too far away from me, I'll blow my whistle.'

I squeeze Chloe's hand back. 'You can do it,' I say. 'You might see a *Caretta caretta*.'

Chloe exhales. 'Okay,' she says. 'Let's go snorkelling.'

We all hold hands as we lower ourselves into the water. I try not to think about the depth we're crossing before we make it to the coral.

Emily taps me on the back and points off to my right. It's a school of tiny shimmery fish.

I raise my head above the surface as Emily pulls out her mouthpiece. 'Did you see how many there were?' she says. 'At least two hundred and fifty.'

We put our faces back in the water and keep kicking. I hear a muffled squeal.

There's a grey and black spotted fish the size of Bella's torso swimming directly underneath her. She bravely reaches out and touches its tail before it disappears.

We all stick our heads up. 'That was the biggest fish I've ever seen,' Bella says. 'But it was so friendly!'

Marnie waves a disposable underwater camera in the air. 'I got a photo,' she says. 'It was a potato cod.'

We float facedown again and watch dozens more fish swim by. Some have black and white stripes, others are blue, and a few seem to sparkle in different shades of yellow.

Phwweeeeeeeet.

I lift up my mask and squint back at Kate. She has one hand on top of the other with her thumbs wriggling out on either side.

'It's the hand signal for turtle!' Chloe squeals. 'Where?'

Kate motions to our left and we all madly kick our flippers.

Mr Martin sees it first. He stretches his arm out in the direction of the turtle.

I'd gasp if my mouthpiece allowed it. It's an enormous turtle, with flippers outstretched,

gliding through the water.

We instinctively stay still, giving it enough space so we don't frighten it away.

I look through the water at Chloe. I can tell by her puffy cheeks that she's beaming. The turtle lingers for about five minutes before swimming away into the dark drop off the edge of the reef.

Phweeeeeeeeeeet.

Our heads bob up again.

'Time's up!' Kate calls. 'We've got to get back for breakfast!'

Chloe paddles over to Marnie and gives her a hug. 'Thank you so much!' she says. 'It was a *Caretta caretta*! An adult male!'

Marnie's smile grows even bigger than Chloe's. 'And now is the perfect time to tell you I had a call from Dr Meyer,' she says. 'Cameron pulled through. Dr Meyer's never seen it happen before. She says Cameron will be back in the ocean soon.'

We all squeal – except for Mr Martin, who pumps his fists.

'Forget the regatta, this is a true victory, Chloe,' I say. 'You're a champion.'

She wipes a happy tear from her eye. 'We did it together,' she says. 'Team Anti-Princess.'

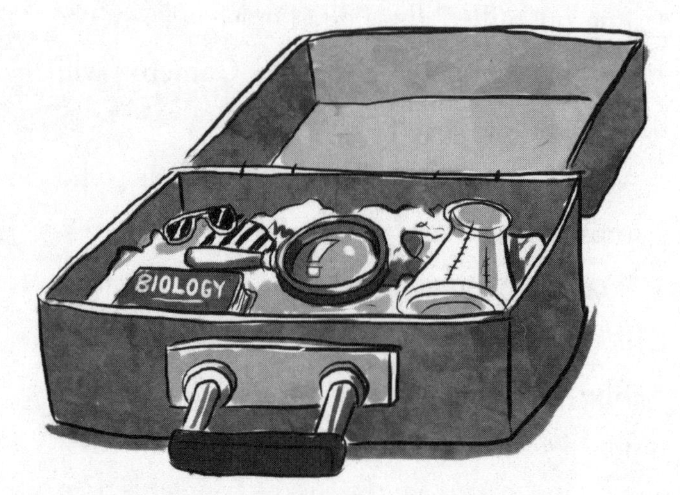

Swimsuit, check.

Pyjamas, check.

Magnifying glass, check.

Beaker, check.

'I bet you're the only person who brought a beaker and a magnifying glass on the cruise, Chloe,' Grace says.

I zip my suitcase. 'I had to throw in a few science tools,' I say. 'I wish I could've brought my telescope for the stargazing last night.'

Emily pulls two canvas bags out from under my bed. 'Aren't you forgetting something?'

The bags are filled with popped balloons from last night's party.

'Should we find a bin to put them in?' Bella asks.

I tie up the handles of each bag so none of the lethal latex falls out. 'Not yet. I want to show these to the captain. Anyone want to come?'

Emily checks her watch. 12pm. 'I've seen her eating lunch at the buffet on level five around this time,' she says. 'Let's go see if we can catch her.'

Emily and I each carry a bag up to level five. Bella and Grace follow.

'That's her,' Emily says.

The captain is sitting at a table surrounded by *Capricorn Princess* crewmembers. She polishes off a glass of orange juice as we edge closer to her table.

'Here, take this.' I pass the bag of balloons to Bella and head to the buffet.

I pour a fresh glass of juice and take it to the captain. 'Would you like another OJ, captain?' I ask, offering her the full glass.

'I don't think I've ever been waited on by a passenger,' she laughs. 'Thank you.'

She takes a sip and points at Emily. 'You're the girl from the harbour,' she says. 'The one who doesn't like princesses.'

Buddy, the crew member we met in the corridor last night, pipes up from across the table. 'I think you'll find she calls herself an anti-princess,' he says. 'She's the president of a club and everything – not unlike the captain of a ship, I'd think.'

'Is that right?' the captain asks, picking her

hat up off the table. 'Nice to meet you, Ms President. I'm Cameron Fanning, the captain. And now I have to get back to work – for a few more hours at least.'

Grace and Bella let out little squeals. Emily giggles.

'Is something funny?' the captain asks.

I nod. I almost can't believe it.

'You have the same name as a turtle we know,' I say.

'A turtle,' she says. 'Now I've heard it all.'

I pull a popped balloon from one of the bags and hold it out in the palm of my hand.

'The funny thing is, we're actually here to talk to you about Cameron,' I say. 'See this squidgy, rubbery thing here? Something like this almost killed her.'

The captain takes it from my hand and rubs it between her fingers.

'It's a balloon,' she says.

'That's right. Cameron swallowed a popped balloon just like that. Lots of turtles swallow them,' I say. 'Cameron was very lucky to survive.'

The captain nods towards the canvas bags we're carrying. 'What else do you have there?'

I open the handles of one of the bags and she peers in.

'Gosh, there are hundreds of balloons in there,' she says. 'Are they from the ship?'

I place the bags beside her feet. 'Yes, I wanted you to take them,' I say. 'And promise that you'll never decorate the ship with balloons again.'

The captain puts on her hat. 'I'll take your suggestion on board,' she says. 'Now, I really must get on with my day.'

She picks up a bag in each hand and tries to get past the anti-princesses. Grace, Bella and Emily step from side to side so that she can't pass.

'I'm sorry, captain,' I say. 'But that's just not good enough.'

'Can someone help me?' she calls out in the direction of the crew members' table.

Marnie jumps up and rushes over with a sly smile. 'Yes, captain?'

'These girls, although very noble in their cause, are in my way,' the captain says.

'I just want to save more turtles from dying,' I say.

The captain rolls her eyes. 'You said your turtle, the one named after me, survived,' she says. 'I'm sorry that it swallowed a balloon, which may or may not have come from my ship, but it didn't kill her.'

My skin starts to tingle. Biologists say it's one of the first signs of anger.

'With all due respect, captain, Cameron was not named after you,' I say. 'I chose Cameron because she's a *Caretta caretta* – Cameron the Caretta – it's called alliteration. And, I'll have you know, the *Caretta caretta* is endangered. They could be extinct in the very near future. And Cameron was very, very lucky. Most turtles that swallow plastic die.'

The captain looks at Marnie.

'She's right, captain,' Marnie says. 'I helped rescue Cameron. She's not the first turtle I've seen in trouble, either.'

The captain puts the bags down and throws her hands up in the air.

'Fine,' she says. 'No more balloons on the *Capricorn Princess* – ever. Dispose of these, Marnie. Good work, anti-princesses – you're a determined bunch, aren't you?'

The captain marches off as Emily, Bella and Grace embrace me in a group hug.

'I'm sorry she was rude,' Marnie says. 'She's not used to being bossed around.'

I slip out from the anti-princesses' arms and hug Marnie.

'It's okay,' I say. 'It's the other Cameron I care about.'

Mission Cameron: complete.

'Ladies and gentlemen, welcome to the Maze Break Summer Showdown!'

The host is a woman with red hair like mine. She's standing on stage in front of ten giant television screens labelled with all the Maze Break finalists' usernames.

'Spectators will be able to watch our Maze Breakers in action on these big screens behind me,' she says. 'The Maze Breakers themselves will be seated in the booths lined up along each side of the gaming room.'

The booths are separated by curtains and each contain a single chair, desk and computer.

'How is this going to work?' Dad whispers.

'Trust me,' I say. 'We'll figure it out.'

The host powers up a digital clock onstage. 1:50pm.

'Maze Breakers, take your places,' she says. 'Competition starts in ten minutes.'

Maximus's blue mohawk bobs up and down through the crowd towards the front booth on the right. Anthony takes the next one along. Some teenagers I haven't seen since the first day on the harbour fill a few more booths.

'I'll wait for the last booth,' I say.

JW, the boy with the braces and fluffy blond moustache who almost figured me out on the deck, takes the second-last booth.

'Okay,' I say. 'I'll get that one next to him.'

I hug the anti-princesses and Dad and walk towards the final empty booth.

It's almost as though I can feel the stares of the other Maze Breakers searing my back. Voices start yelling across the room.

'It's a girl!'

'That can't be right!'

'She's just a kid!'

'They tricked us!'

I smile as if I have no idea what the fuss is about.

'Good luck,' Dad calls out as I take my seat.

JW rips open the curtain separating our booths. 'I knew it!' he yells. 'A real mathematician knows there's no such thing as luck in maths!'

I shrug my shoulders.

'Real mathematicians don't make wild assumptions either,' I say. 'Like assuming my Dad was the Maze Breaker for no logical reason.'

JW laughs. 'I'm Jake Walmsley, by the way,' he says. 'Jake_can_break17.'

He closes the curtain.

I look back at the anti-princesses and motion for them to join me.

'It will be like a team effort,' I say as they form a tight semicircle around the entrance to the booth.

'Part one of Mission Maze Break complete,' I say. 'Now for part two.'

I hear a crew member's voice from the other side of the anti-princesses. 'Is everything okay in there?' she asks. 'It looks a little squishy.'

'All good,' I call out. 'It's just my cheer squad.'

Beep, beep, beep.

'Maze Breakers, begin!'

My pigeon avatar pops up on screen.

'There we are,' Grace says. 'The big screen in the middle.'

The anti-princesses have their backs to me and are watching the screens on stage.

I concentrate on moving my pigeon through the maze. I hit a dead end within four seconds. I backtrack, doing my best to remember the turns I take along the way. I hit the same dead end again.

'Keep calm,' I whisper. 'As long as you don't take the same path more than twice you should find your way out in good time.'

I take a right turn, then a left, then another right. I hit another dead end. 'Remember Trémaux's Algorithm,' I whisper. 'Turn around and go back. It's simple.'

I turn left, then right, then left, then left again.

The host's voice booms over the microphone. 'Jake_can_break17 has broken the maze.'

I keep my eyes on the pigeon. Jake still has to crack the maths problem.

The host's voice calls out again: 'Lin2win has broken the maze.'

I take a right turn. There's a clearing up ahead. I move my pigeon straight through it.

'AP23 has broken the maze.'

The anti-princesses clap.

'Not yet,' I say. 'I have to solve the problem.'

A new screen flashes up on the monitor.

01100010 01101001 01110100 01110011
00100000 01101001 01101110 00100000
01100001 00100000 01100010 01111001
01110100 01100101

'It's binary code,' Bella whispers. 'You'll figure this out for sure, Emily.'

There are only two numbers in binary code, 0 and 1, and when you count using binary you start with 0, then 1, then start back at 0 again but add a 1 on the left. So, 0=0, 1=1, 2=10, 3=11, 4=100, 5=101, 6=110, 7=111, 8=1000, 9=1001, and 10=1010.

I convert the code on the screen.

```
01100010 = 98
01101001 = 105
01110100 = 116
01110011 = 115
00100000 = 32
01101001 = 105
01101110 = 110
00100000 = 32
01100001 = 97
00100000 = 32
01100010 = 98
01111001 = 121
01110100 = 116
01100101 = 101
```

'Finished!' a voice yells from across the room. It's Lin2win.

The host's voice follows. 'I'm afraid you're not finished until the computer tells you it's game over. Keep going.'

I check my numbers. I can't see any mistakes, but I'm not getting a 'game over' message.

I click a red button at the bottom of the screen and a second window pops up.

'What's that?' Grace asks.

It's a chart full of hundreds of numbers and letters. I recognise it straight away. 'It's an ASCII table,' I say. 'I need to convert the numbers to letters.'

ASCII stands for American Standard Code for Information Interchange – every computer programmer knows it's the code that represents computer text.

I match my numbers to the characters in the table as quickly as I can:

98=b
105=i
116=t
115=s
32=space

105=i
110=n
32=space
97=a
32=space

98=b
121=y
116=t
101=e

'Bits in a byte.'

I slam my finger down on the 8 on my keyboard. 'There are eight bits in a byte!' I yell.

GAME OVER

The anti-princesses are cheering.

I can hardly hear the host announce: 'AP23 is the first to finish! AP23 is the winner of the Maze Break Summer Showdown!'

Jake pulls back the curtain. 'Congratulations,' he says. 'Beaten by a girl – again.'

Before I can ask what he means, the anti-princesses have me in the tightest group hug of all time.

'Time to come up on stage, AP23,' the host calls over the microphone. 'Whoever you are.'

The crowd parts to make a path for me.

'I can't believe we got beaten by a girl,' Maximus says as I walk past.

'I bet her dad helped her,' says another voice I don't recognise.

I clench my fists and ignore them.

A crew member side-stage says: 'Meet Billy27, the creator of Maze Break.'

I turn in a full circle searching for Billy27.

The only person on stage is the host of the showdown.

'Where is he?' I ask.

The host cocks her head to one side.

'Do I need to spell it out to you of all people?' she asks. 'It's me.'

I cover my mouth with both hands. I can feel the blood rushing to my face and my skin heating up. 'I'm so sorry. I just thought Billy was a man's name...I'm so, so sorry.'

She smiles. 'It can be a male or female name. As for the 27, it's my favourite number because it's the only number that is three times the sum of its digits – cool, huh?'

I want to crawl into a hole and hide. I'm so embarrassed for assuming the Maze Break creator was a man. And to think I was so angry the other Maze Breakers assumed Dad was the gamer instead of me!

Billy brings the microphone to her mouth and addresses the crowd. 'May I present to you the winner of the Maze Break Summer

Showdown – AP23,' she says. 'Otherwise known as eleven-year-old Emily Martin.'

'Imposter!' a voice calls out from the crowd.

'Rematch!' calls another.

Billy points and shakes her finger as if she's a teacher speaking to misbehaving students.

'Some of you seem to be quite ignorant,' she says. 'Put your hand up if you've ever been beaten by a player called Billy27 in Zombie Spat, Hammer Man or any other online game?'

Jake's hand goes up first. The rest of the Maze Breakers follow.

'Well, you've been beaten by a girl many times over, because Billy27 is me,' she says.

The Maze Breakers slowly put their hands down. Some hang their heads.

'As everyone knows, I created Maze Break a year ago and it has become one of the country's most popular games,' Billy says. 'But, today you played the final round of Maze Break – ever.'

The room goes silent.

'The truth is, the showdown was an elaborate

ploy by me to find the next generation of the world's best coders with strong maths skills and an interest in gaming,' Billy says. 'So, if you're willing, Emily, your prize is the opportunity to come up with a new concept for a game that we can develop together…something that will be even bigger and better than Maze Break.'

Billy pushes the microphone in front of my face for an answer. I fight the urge to squeal with excitement.

'I'd love to do that,' I say. 'I already know what the game will be called.'

Billy smiles. 'Do tell.'

'It will be called the Anti-Princess Club,' I say. 'Anyone can play it – boys or girls – but there'll be one main rule: the anti-princesses won't need rescuing.'

Bella, Chloe and Grace start chanting at the top of their lungs. '*We don't need rescuing!*'

Billy leans in and whispers, 'Let's do it.'

Mission Maze Break: complete.

EPILOGUE

I've spent almost the entire summer holiday working on the *Anti-Princess Club* video game with Billy27. There are four avatars to choose from based on me, Chloe, Bella and Grace, and their missions will be just like the ones our club has actually completed in real life: building a treehouse, launching rockets, winning soccer tournaments...it's going to be so much fun.

Speaking of fun stuff, Bella heard back from Ant's parents. They made the anti-princess doll prototypes and got a bunch of random kids to play with them. The verdict was – they LOVED them. Now, the dolls are being made in a factory and their first stop will be the shelves of the *Capricorn Princess* gift shop.

Ant has started a sailing blog that uses lots of slightly obscure nautical terms like 'stanchion' and 'turnbuckle'. I think he's still trying to redeem himself after his poor sailing performance. Grace has moved on. She's learning how to abseil now.

And Marnie contacted Chloe to let her know Cameron was fully rehabilitated. Cameron was still too young for Dr Meyer to tell whether she was male or female – but the most important thing is she set Cameron free into the open ocean after two months. When word got around about *Capricorn Princess* banning balloons, other ships followed its lead.

On top of it all, I met Maze Breaker Lin2win's sister on the dock at Fremantle. Her name is Willow and she's eleven, just like us. She was onboard for the showdown and loved the idea of the Anti-Princess Club so much that she asked if she could start a west coast chapter. Of course I said yes, as long as she remembers one thing: 'We don't need rescuing.'

ACTIVITIES

Hi, everyone! It's Emily here, president of the Anti-Princess Club.

Bella, Grace, Chloe and I love the summer holidays – there's so much time for gaming, experiments, days at the beach, stargazing and official Anti-Princess Club missions.

On the topic of missions, I hope you're ready for some of your own. We have written down a few of our favourite summer activities, and we want you to use them to have the best summer ever!

TTYL!

Emily, Bella, Grace, Chloe X

WHICH ANTI-PRINCESS ARE YOU?

1 **The first thing you do when you wake up in the morning is...**

A Turn on your computer

B Draw a picture of what you dreamt about

C Stretch

D Check the sky with your telescope

2 **The thing you love most about school is...**

A The computers

B Art lessons

C Sport/PE

D Science projects

3 **If you could change the world in just one way, you would...**

A Invent a crack-proof way to stop internet fraud

B Design a bed that makes itself

C Hold the Olympic Games annually

D Cure disease

4 Your biggest weakness is…

A Becoming a little too easily outraged

B Daydreaming too often

C Not being able to sit still

D Enjoying grossing people out

5 You most admire…

A Ada Lovelace – mathematician and the world's first computer programmer

B Frida Kahlo – artist

C Ellyse Perry – international cricketer and footballer

D Jane Goodall – primatologist/ethologist/ chimpanzee expert

Turn the page for your results…

If you answered mostly A – You are just like Emily! You're a natural leader who stands up for what you believe in. You inspire others with your strong sense of justice and willingness to defend what's right. You're loud, outspoken and not afraid to let the world know when you're angry. You love computers and numbers. Most of all, you love your friends.

If you answered mostly B – You are just like Bella! You're a dreamer with big ideas and visions for how everything should work and look. You have artistic flair. You're also great with your hands and can build just about anything you set your mind to. You'd love to invent something that would change kids' lives for the better.

If you answered mostly C – You are just like Grace! You can't sit still. You're a natural-born athlete who excels at anything physical. You love all sports – but you're not content to spectate, you have to participate. You're a competitor, but also gracious in defeat. You're also patient and understand that reaching big goals takes hard work and lots of time.

If you answered mostly D – You are just like Chloe! You're a scientist who is always on a quest to know more. You're an explorer who is desperate to travel the world and the universe. You get bored easily and you're itching to tackle the world's big mysteries – curing diseases, reversing pollution, discovering new species. But you don't take life too seriously – you're a prankster with a fondness for toilet humour.

EMILY

Ada Lovelace

Born: 10 December 1815, London,
United Kingdom

Why she is my anti-princess heroine:
Ada grew up in a time when girls
really were treated like princesses
who couldn't do anything by
themselves. Girls were expected to
wear big frilly dresses and sit around
being pretty, but Ada became a
brilliant mathematician instead. When
Ada was 28, she wrote the first
computer program - before there
was even a computer that could run
it. Talk about a mathematics genius!

MISSION: BINARY BRACELETS

Letter	Binary	Letter	Binary
A	0100 0001	N	0100 1110
B	0100 0010	O	0100 1111
C	0100 0011	P	0101 0000
D	0100 0100	Q	0101 0001
E	0100 0101	R	0101 0010
F	0100 0110	S	0101 0011
G	0100 0111	T	0101 0100
H	0100 1000	U	0101 0101
I	0100 1001	V	0101 0110
J	0100 1010	W	0101 0111
K	0100 1011	X	0101 1000
L	0100 1100	Y	0101 1001
M	0100 1101	Z	0101 1010

As you saw in the Maze Break showdown, I know a little bit about binary code. Binary code is the language that computers use to send and receive information. There are only two numbers in binary, 0 and 1, but you can use it to write words – like the puzzle in the Maze Break final showdown.

Binary is kind of like a secret code, but don't worry – you've got all the tools you need to crack it.

You'll need:

- beads in three different colours (for 0s, 1s, and spaces)
- string

Figure out what you want to put on your bracelet and use the table to work out what it would be in binary. I used my initials – E M – which is 01000101 01001101.

Tie a knot in one end of the string so that the beads won't slip off.

Put your beads on the string with a single space bead between the letters and two space beads to show the beginning and the end.

I used black beads for 0, white beads for 1, and grey beads for spaces, so my bracelet looks like this:

MISSION: DESIGN YOUR OWN MAZE

It's pretty obvious that I love games and puzzles, and especially mazes. Luckily it's really easy to create your own maze. Maybe you and your anti-princess friends can host your own Maze Break tournament – make sure you make your maze extra tricky!

You'll need:

- a pencil
- a pen
- an eraser
- a piece of paper

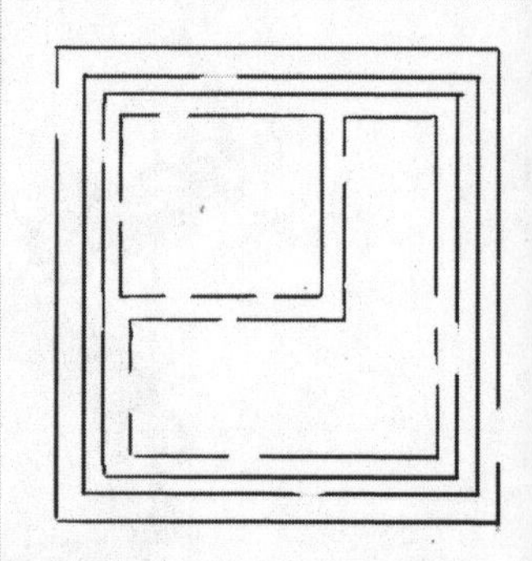

1 In pencil, draw one big square that will be the edge of your maze, and erase two holes in it – one for the entry, and one for the exit. Draw a few squares inside the main one and erase two or three holes in each of those as well.

2 Add a few smaller shapes inside the maze – a small square and a couple of rectangles works well. Fill those with shapes, and erase two or three holes in each shape you draw.

 In pencil, lightly draw a single path through the maze – this is the solution to your maze. Now you can start making it complicated by drawing lines to close off any path other than the one you've chosen. If you want to make it a bit more difficult, you can erase more holes in the squares – and so make more dead-end paths!

4 Go over your maze walls in pen, and erase the path you drew in step 3. Congrats – you just designed your first maze!

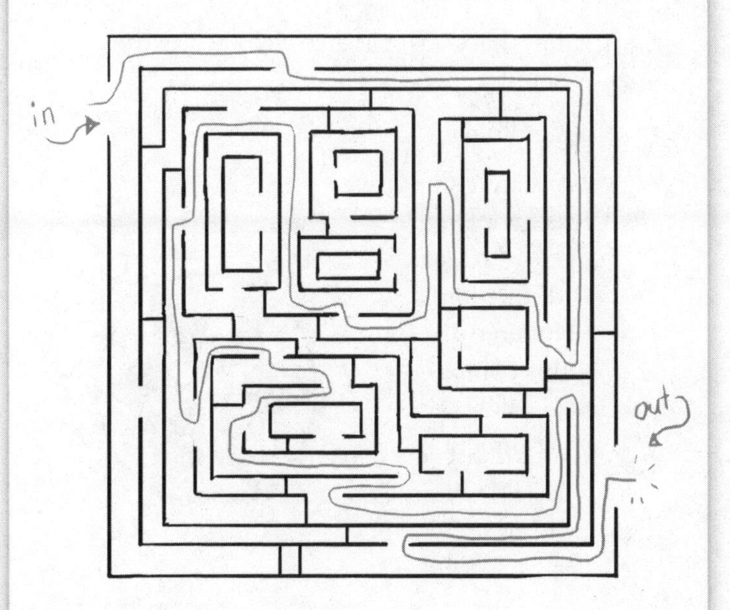

MISSION: RANDOM WALK GAME

Have you ever played Marco Polo in the pool? Or Blind Man's Bluff? The Random Walk game is kind of like these two mixed together – plus a little bit of mathematical theory, of course.

A 'random walk' is the path that something would take if each step was random, so in this game we use dice to tell us where to go. The aim is for the person who is 'It' to catch another player – and the challenge is that no one knows where they're going!

You'll need:

- a die (that's a single dice) for each player except the person who's 'It'
- a blindfold
- a 6-point compass rose on a large piece of paper, with the points numbered 1–6 – this compass rose will show what direction each die roll allows a player to move in

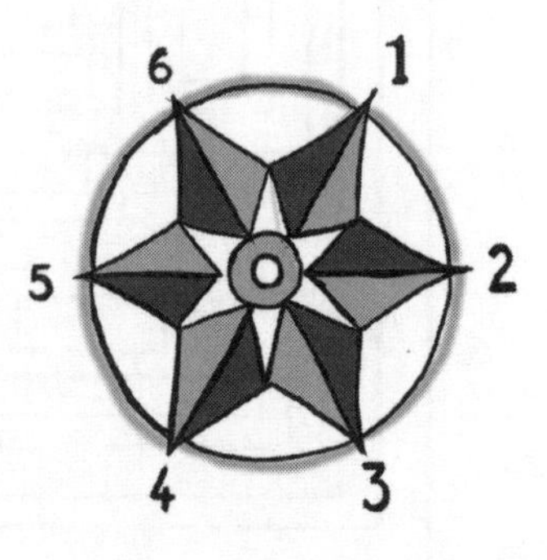

 Stick the compass rose on the wall, or nominate a player to be the 'Navigator'. The Navigator will call out what direction a player can go in after they roll.

 The player with the next birthday is 'It' and they stand in the middle with the blindfold on.

3 The other players take a die each and pick a spot anywhere in the area.

4 Play starts with the youngest player. Each player rolls their die and takes one step in the direction shown on the compass rose.

 Once all the players have taken a step, It takes TWO steps in any direction they choose.

6 This continues until It catches someone. The caught player becomes the new It and it starts all over again!

(If you had a Navigator, then the caught player becomes the new Navigator and the Navigator becomes the new It.)

If you want to make it a little easier, before It takes their steps, they call out 'anti!' and each player has to respond with 'princess!'

BELLA

Frida Kahlo

Born: 6 July 1907, Coyoacán, Mexico City, Mexico

Why she is my anti-princess heroine:
When Frida was 18, she was in a terrible bus accident that meant she had to stay in bed for months recovering. Although Frida found it hard to get better, instead of waiting for somebody to rescue her, she decided to start painting. She was an amazing painter, and is still one of the most celebrated painters in the world.

MISSION: BUILD A BOAT

Summer is my favourite season – I get to spend loads of time outside sketching and building awesome creations, like the super-fast billycart I once entered into a derby, and the Anti-Princess Club headquarters – AKA a treehouse with its own planetarium. I love building things – especially things that go fast! – and Chloe, Grace, Emily and I have so much fun racing milk bottle sailboats. I've got a few tips for you to make your own boats for your next mission.

You'll need:

- a plastic or cardboard milk carton
- thick paper
- a peg
- scissors
- glue or tape

1. Cut your milk carton in half lengthwise – this will be the hull of your boat. Be careful not to cut extra holes in the carton or it won't float!

2. Cut a medium-sized triangle out of the thick paper – this is going to be your sail.

3. Punch a hole in two opposite sides of the sail and poke the straw through the holes.

4. Clip a peg to the bottom of the straw, and glue the peg into the boat.

5. If you want, decorate your milk carton – but remember, it's going to get wet!

MISSION: DESIGN A TREEHOUSE

I designed the Anti-Princess Club HQ and – with some help from my parents and my anti-princess best friends – built it in my backyard. I've drawn a picture of the tree in my yard on a grid, and I'll show you how to scale it so you can draw it on a bigger piece of paper and come up with your own amazing treehouse. Here's your chance to design your own club HQ!

You'll need:

- a large piece of paper
- a pencil
- an eraser
- a ruler

1. Copy the grid pattern that I've drawn onto your piece of paper, but make each square 4 x 4cm. The easiest way to do this is to draw a border of dots 4cm apart along the edge of your paper, and then connect the dots with lines across your paper. Tada – a grid! (Make sure your grid has the same number of squares as mine – 5 across, 7 down.)

Now that you have the grid, you can start drawing the tree. Each square on the grid is like a little picture, and if you copy each little picture they make up the whole tree – pretty neat, huh? So pick a square on my grid and the same square on your grid and start drawing!

3. Once you've copied the whole tree, you can start designing your very own treehouse on top of it! I've drawn my first treehouse design here for inspiration.

TIP: If you want to design a few treehouses, you can go over your tree in marker so that you can erase each treehouse you draw without losing the tree.

MISSION: CHALKBOARD CREATION

I love art. I carry around a sketchpad ALL. THE. TIME. Sometimes I like to draw really BIG pictures that don't fit in my sketchpad, so I have a big chalkboard in my room for when inspiration strikes! It's super easy to make your own – you might need a little help with the painting, so make sure your parents are around when you're planning for this mission.

You'll need:

- fibreboard (or something similar like plywood) cut to size
- primer paint
- chalkboard paint
- a paint roller or large flat brush

(If you don't have these items at home, head to your local hardware store for supplies!)

Paint a coat of primer on your fibreboard and let it dry. The primer makes your chalkboard paint easier to apply and write on.

Apply two even coats of chalkboard paint. Don't forget to let your paint dry between each coat.

Tada – you've got a chalkboard!

TIP: You can leave a bit of a border around the edge of your painted area to look like a frame for your chalkboard. You can even decorate it – maybe with some shells from the beach, or paper flowers! Hmmm… I think I'll make a new chalkboard, too, and design some awesome summer decorations for the frame.

GRACE

Ellyse Perry

Born: 3 November 1990, Wahroonga, New South Wales

Why she is my anti-princess heroine:
Ellyse was the first person to represent Australia in soccer and cricket at the same time – and she was only sixteen! A lot of people say that Ellyse shouldn't play two sports – that she should focus on one instead – but she's not letting anyone tell her what to do. She currently plays cricket for the New South Wales Breakers and soccer for Sydney FC. If only she played for the Newcastle Jets!

MISSION: BEACH RELAY

Summer is a great season for sports – especially surfing and beach cricket – so on hot summer days we head to the beach and go swimming and exploring. Chloe loves the rock pools, but I prefer the surf – except when I get jellyfish on my head!

You've probably figured out that I'm a pretty fast runner. And I'm not trying to brag, I'm just being honest. But my favourite thing about relay races is that it doesn't matter if one person is a really fast runner because winning the race is about working together as a team.

You'll need:

- beach bags
- long skirts – grass skirts are the best, but any will work
- big shorts from your parents
- sunglasses
- summer hats
- flower leis or long necklaces
- beach chairs

1. Split up into teams of two or more and fill each bag with a skirt, hat, flower lei/necklace, a pair of shorts, and sunglasses.
2. Mark a starting line in the sand and place your beach bags on the ground a metre apart. Walk 20 steps away from the starting line and put your beach chairs here.
3. Have each team line up behind their beach bag. Once everyone is ready, start the relay race by yelling, 'Surf's up!'
4. The first player in the line should take all the items out of their beach bag, put them on, run to the beach chair, sit down, stand back up, run back to their team, remove all of the items, and hand them to next person in line, who starts putting them on – whew!
5. The first team to have everyone run the relay (with all the clothes on!) wins.

MISSION: SALUTE THE SUN

Sport is basically my life – I love running, I play soccer and cricket, I surf, I ride, and anything else to get moving. I like to do yoga in the morning – when my three brothers aren't bothering me! I've drawn a few pictures of my favourite yoga poses. When you put them together like this, it's called a 'sun salutation'. So here's your mission – go and salute the sun with some yoga in your backyard.

MISSION: SLIP 'N' SLIDE

Sometimes the best fun is had in your backyard with a hose, a bit of tarp, and some soap. Don't believe me? Try it out for yourself in this mission – I promise you'll have fun.

You'll need:

- tarpaulin
- a hose
- liquid soap

1 Clear out a long strip of backyard for your slide. Make sure there are no rocks or sticks in there to slide over – I know we're not princesses, but trust me, sliding over rocks and twigs is not fun for your bum!

 Lay your tarp down and squirt a good amount of soap at the end closest to the hose.

 Start running the hose on the tarp and wait for the soap to get nice and bubbly – give it a rub with your hands or feet if you get impatient.

 Take a good run-up at the soapy end of the tarp and slide!

The slide works really well on a bit of a hill – or an incline, as Emily would say – but it is loads of fun on the flat too.

CHLOE

Jane Goodall

Born: 3 April 1934, London, United Kingdom

Why she is my anti-princess heroine:
Jane undertook a fifty-five-year study of wild chimpanzees in Tanzania – can you imagine studying something for fifty-five years?! Jane didn't have any scientific training at the time, but she still learnt new and amazing things about the wild chimpanzees – and she's still the only human who has ever been accepted into a group of chimpanzees. Perhaps I can spend a summer studying the Caretta caretta – maybe I'll even see Cameron the Caretta again!

MISSION: NIGHT SKY KOURABIEDES

Yiayia and I love making kourabiedes, especially in the summer holidays. Yiayia says kourabiedes remind her of Christmas in Greece because everyone makes them for special occasions. I treat cooking like a science experiment, so I changed the traditional recipe a little bit – but Yiayia and I agree that these kourabiedes are stellar! I've written the recipe down for you to try out.

TOOLS:

- electric beater
- non-stick baking paper
- tablespoon
- star-shaped cookie cutter
- baking tray
- cooling rack
- teaspoon
- mixing bowl

INGREDIENTS:

250g butter
1 egg
300g plain flour
100g chopped almonds
Sifted icing sugar to dust
120g icing sugar
1 tsp vanilla extract
½ tsp baking powder
20 whole cloves

METHOD:

1. Ask your parents to preheat the oven to 160°C, while you line a large baking tray with non-stick baking paper.

2. Use an electric beater to beat the butter in a large bowl until it's pale and creamy. Add the icing sugar and egg yolk. Beat until well mixed.
3. Fold in the flour until it's just mixed, and then stir in the almonds.
4. Split your mixture in half – one half will be your moons, the other half will be stars.
5. Scoop out tablespoons of the mixture and roll them into balls. Lightly flour a board and roll the balls into 8cm lengths on a lightly floured surface. Shape them into crescents and place on the tray.
6. Get the other half of your mixture and press it on the floured board (with your hands or a rolling pin) until it's about 2cm thick. Cut cookies out of the mixture with a star-shaped cookie cutter, then place on the tray with your crescent-shaped cookies. Insert a clove into the centre of each biscuit.
7. Bake for 15–20 minutes or until the cookies are gold in colour. Ask your parents to pull them out of the oven, and then place them on a cooling rack. Be careful – they'll be hot!
8. Sprinkle with a little icing sugar, and when they're completely cooled, add a generous dusting of icing sugar.

MISSION: BLAST-OFF 2.0

You might remember when my new teacher Mr Ashton tried to give me a spew-worthy science project making perfume – but I made a rocket out of bicarb soda and vinegar (and rotten eggs!) instead. I've outlined my method here so you can create your own rocket with a bit of help from your parents. There's a bit of chemistry and a bit of physics involved in this experiment, so I know you're going to have a blast.

TOOLS: (for the rocket and the launcher)

- a plastic soft-drink bottle
- cardboard
- rubber band
- a pin
- a bamboo skewer
- scissors
- thick paper
- duct tape
- an uninflated balloon
- a straw

INGREDIENTS: (for the fuel)

- Vinegar (you can use any kind, but I use white vinegar)
- 3 tbsp bicarbonate of soda
- Cling wrap

METHOD:

PREPARING YOUR ROCKET

1. Roll your thick paper into a cone shape and cut the bottom so it's even. Tape this cone to the bottom of the bottle. (The cone reduces air resistance and will make your rocket go faster.)

2. Cut 4 triangles out of your cardboard for your rocket fins. Tape these to the neck of the bottle. (If you bend one side of your triangle so it's perpendicular to the rest, it will be much easier to tape onto the bottle.)

3. Tape a straw to the side of your rocket. (This will be placed on the skewer and help the rocket launch.)

PREPARING YOUR LAUNCHER

Place the skewer in the ground outside – you can either stand it up straight or on a 45-degree angle. If it's straight, the rocket will go upwards, and if it's on an angle then the rocket will follow that angle.

PREPARING YOUR FUEL

5. Fill your bottle about ¼ full with vinegar.

6. Put the bicarb soda into a large square of cling wrap, fold the corners up like a knapsack and twist them together tightly. (This will slowly unravel after you put it in the bottle, giving you time to stand well clear of the rocket before it blasts off.)

7. Poke a small hole in the top of your balloon (the part that expands when you inflate it) with a pin. When the rocket launches, the fuel will be released out of this hole.

8. Carefully put the bicarb soda parcel in the bottle – try not to move the bottle too much or you could cause the cling wrap to unravel and it might go off in your hands!

9. Put the balloon over the neck of the bottle and secure it with a rubber band.

GETTING READY FOR LIFT OFF

Carefully place the rocket onto the launcher by sliding the straw over the skewer. Make sure the fins are on the ground and the cone is pointing upwards.

It will take a few seconds for the bicarb soda and the vinegar to mix and react, so stand back and get ready for blast-off!

SCIENTIFIC EXPLANATION

When the bicarb soda (a bicarbonate) and the vinegar (an acid) mix together, they create carbon dioxide (a gas). The carbon dioxide fills up the empty space in the rocket causing pressure inside the bottle. The gas has to escape somewhere, so it forces the fuel out of the rocket through the balloon. This force causes the rocket to lift off the ground.

MISSION:
SNOT SCIENTISTS

I love making sticky, icky fake snot and grossing out my brother Alex so much that I just have to share my own special recipe with you. When you're done, stick it to your nostril and freak people right out!

TOOLS:

- heat-proof bowl
- teaspoon
- fork
- measuring cup

INGREDIENTS:

- ½ cup very hot water (you should ask your parents to boil the kettle)
- 3 tsp gelatine
- ¼ cup golden syrup (you can probably use any type of syrup from the supermarket)
- Green food colouring

METHOD:

1. Pour hot water into the bowl.
2. Add gelatine.
3. Wait for the mixture to become soft.
4. Mix with your fork.
5. Add golden syrup.
6. Mix with your fork again.

7. Add a tiny drop of green food colouring (substitute for yellow if you want to make fake pus).

8. Mix with your fork again until long, tendril-like strands form.

9. Pop the mixture into the fridge for up to half an hour.

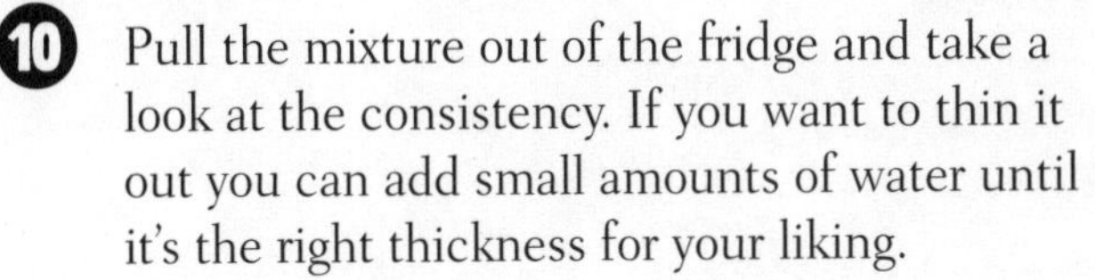

10. Pull the mixture out of the fridge and take a look at the consistency. If you want to thin it out you can add small amounts of water until it's the right thickness for your liking.

SCIENTIFIC EXPLANATION

Mucus – your real snot – is made up of proteins and sugars that combine to form long, stretchy, sticky chains. Although gelatine is a different kind of protein, it combines with the syrup in a similar way to make the fake snot. The long, tendril-like strands that you saw in your fake snot are protein strands, and that's what makes the snot so sticky and stretchy.

Read the other adventures of THE ANTI-PRINCESS CLUB

Samantha Turnbull is an author, blogger and award-winning journalist. Samantha doesn't like stories about damsels in distress. Instead, she loves to read and write stories about strong girls who don't need rescuing. The Anti-Princess Club books are her debut novels.

antiprincessclub.com.au

samanthaturnbull.com.au

Sarah Davis spends most of her days scheming up new ideas and making a mess with paint – she is definitely most like Bella. She taught herself how to draw and paint, and has been illustrating award-winning books since 2008. She has illustrated more than thirty books for publishers in Australia and overseas.

sarah-davis.org